Good-bye, Mr. Chips

&

To You, Mr. Chips

By

James Hilton

Cover Photograph: Jase Curtis

ISBN: 978-1-78139-161-7

Contents

Good-bye, Mr. Chips

To You, Mr. Chips

i

Good-bye, Mr. Chips

James Hilton

1

When you are getting on in years (but not ill, of course), you get very sleepy at times, and the hours seem to pass like lazy cattle moving across a landscape. It was like that for Chips as the autumn term progressed and the days shortened till it was actually dark enough to light the gas before call-over. For Chips, like some old sea captain, still measured time by the signals of the past; and well he might, for he lived at Mrs. Wickett's, just across the road from the School. He had been there more than a decade, ever since he finally gave up his mastership; and it was Brookfield far more than Greenwich time that both he and his landlady kept. "Mrs. Wickett," Chips would sing out, in that jerky, high-pitched voice that had still a good deal of sprightliness in it, "you might bring me a cup of tea before prep, will you?"

When you are getting on in years it is nice to sit by the fire and drink a cup of tea and listen to the school bell sounding dinner, call-over, prep, and lights-out. Chips always wound up the clock after that last bell; then he put the wire guard in front of the fire, turned out the gas, and carried a detective novel to bed. Rarely did he read more than a page of it before sleep came swiftly and peacefully, more like a mystic intensifying of perception than any changeful entrance into another world. For his days and nights were equally full of dreaming.

He was getting on in years (but not ill, of course); indeed, as Doctor Merivale said, there was really nothing the matter with him. "My dear fellow, you're fitter than I am," Merivale would say, sipping a glass of sherry when he called every fortnight or so. "You're past the age when people get these horrible diseases; you're one of the few lucky ones who're going to die a really natural death. That is, of course, if you die at all. You're such a remarkable old boy that one never knows." But when Chips had a cold or when east winds roared over the fenlands, Merivale would sometimes take Mrs. Wickett aside in the lobby and whisper: "Look after him, you know. His chest . . . it puts a strain on his heart. Nothing really wrong with him--only *anno domini*, but that's the most fatal complaint of all, in the end."

Anno domini . . . by Jove, yes. Born in 1848, and taken to the Great Exhibition as a toddling child--not many people still alive could boast a thing like that. Besides, Chips could even remember Brookfield in Wetherby's time. A phenomenon, that was. Wetherby had been an old man in those days--1870--easy to remember because of the Franco-Prussian War. Chips had put in for Brookfield after a year at Melbury, which he hadn't liked, because he had been ragged there a good deal. But Brookfield he had liked, almost from the beginning. He remembered that day of his preliminary interview--sunny June, with the air full of flower scents and the plick-plock of cricket on the pitch. Brookfield was playing Barnhurst, and one of the Barnhurst boys, a chubby little fellow, made a brilliant century. Queer that a thing like that should stay in the memory so clearly. Wetherby himself was very fatherly and courteous; he must have been ill then, poor chap, for he died during the summer vacation, before Chips began his first term. But the two had seen and spoken to each other, anyway.

Chips often thought, as he sat by the fire at Mrs. Wickett's: I am probably the only man in the world who has a vivid recollection of old Wetherby. . . . Vivid, yes; it was a frequent picture in his mind, that summer day with the sunlight filtering through the dust in Wetherby's study. "You are a young man, Mr. Chipping, and Brookfield is an old foundation. Youth and age often combine well. Give your enthusiasm to Brookfield, and Brookfield will give you something in return. And don't let anyone play tricks with you. I--er--gather that discipline was not always your strong point at Melbury?"

"Well, no, perhaps not, sir."

"Never mind; you're full young; it's largely a matter of experience. You have another chance here. Take up a firm attitude from the beginning--that's the secret of it."

Perhaps it was. He remembered that first tremendous ordeal of taking prep; a September sunset more than half a century ago; Big Hall full of lusty barbarians ready to pounce on him as their legitimate prey. His youth, fresh-complexioned, high-collared, and side-whiskered (odd fashions people followed in those days), at the mercy of five hundred unprincipled ruffians to whom the baiting of new masters was a fine art, an exciting sport, and something of a tradition. Decent little beggars individually, but, as a mob, just pitiless and implacable. The sudden hush as he took his place at the desk on the dais; the scowl he

4

assumed to cover his inward nervousness; the tall clock ticking behind him, and the smells of ink and varnish; the last blood-red rays slanting in slabs through the stained-glass windows. Someone dropped a desk lid. Quickly, he must take everyone by surprise; he must show that there was no nonsense about him. "You there in the fifth row--you with the red hair--what's your name?"

"Colley, sir."

"Very well, Colley, you have a hundred lines."

No trouble at all after that. He had won his first round.

And years later, when Colley was an alderman of the City of London and a baronet and various other things, he sent his son (also red-haired) to Brookfield, and Chips would say: "Colley, your father was the first boy I ever punished when I came here twenty-five years ago. He deserved it then, and you deserve it now." How they all laughed; and how Sir Richard laughed when his son wrote home the story in next Sunday's letter!

And again, years after that, many years after that, there was an even better joke. For another Colley had just arrived--son of the Colley who was a son of the first Colley. And Chips would say, punctuating his remarks with that little "umph-um" that had by then become a habit with him: "Colley, you are--umph--a splendid example of--umph--inherited traditions. I remember your grandfather--umph--he could never grasp the Ablative Absolute. A stupid fellow, your grandfather. And your father, too--umph--I remember him--he used to sit at that far desk by the wall--he wasn't much better, either. But I do believe--my dear Colley ;that you are--umph--the biggest fool of the lot!" Roars of laughter.

A great joke, this growing old--but a sad joke, too, in a way. And as Chips sat by his fire with autumn gales rattling the windows, the waves of humor and sadness swept over him very often until tears fell, so that when Mrs. Wickett came in with his cup of tea she did not know whether he had been laughing or crying. And neither did Chips himself.

2

Across the road behind a rampart of ancient elms lay Brookfield, russet under its autumn mantle of creeper. A group of eighteenth-century buildings centred upon a quadrangle, and there were acres of playing fields beyond; then came the small dependent village and the open fen country. Brookfield, as Wetherby had said, was an old foundation; established in the reign of Elizabeth, as a grammar school, it might, with better luck, have become as famous as Harrow. Its luck, however, had been not so good; the School went up and down, dwindling almost to non-existence at one time, becoming almost illustrious at another. It was during one of these latter periods, in the reign of the first George, that the main structure had been rebuilt and large additions made. Later, after the Napoleonic Wars and until mid-Victorian days, the School declined again, both in numbers and in repute. Wetherby, who came in 1840, restored its fortunes somewhat; but its subsequent history never raised it to front-rank status. It was, nevertheless, a good school of the second rank. Several notable families supported it; it supplied fair samples of the history-making men of the age--judges, members of parliament, colonial administrators, a few peers and bishops. Mostly, however, it turned out merchants, manufacturers, and professional men, with a good sprinkling of country squires and parsons. It was the sort of school which, when mentioned, would sometimes make snobbish people confess that they rather thought they had heard of it.

But if it had not been this sort of school it would probably not have taken Chips. For Chips, in any social or academic sense, was just as respectable, but no more brilliant, than Brookfield itself.

It had taken him some time to realize this, at the beginning. Not that he was boastful or conceited, but he had been, in his early twenties, as ambitious as most other young men at such an age. His dream had been to get a headship eventually, or at any rate a senior mastership in a really first-class school; it was only gradually, after repeated trials and failures, that he realized the inadequacy of his qualifications. His degree, for instance, was not particularly good, and his discipline, though good enough and improving, was not absolutely reliable under all conditions. He had no private means and no family connections of any importance. About 1880, after he had been at Brookfield a decade, he began to recognize that the odds were heavily against his being able to better himself by moving elsewhere; but about that time, also, the possibility of staying where he was began to fill a comfortable niche in his mind. At forty, he was rooted, settled, and quite happy. At fifty, he was the doyen of the staff. At sixty, under a new and youthful Head, he *was* Brookfield--the guest of honor at Old Brookfeldian dinners, the court of appeal in all matters affecting Brookfield history and traditions. And in 1913, when he turned sixty-five, he retired, was presented with a check and a writing desk and a clock, and went across the road to live at Mrs. Wickett's. A decent career, decently closed; three cheers for old Chips, they all shouted, at that uproarious end-of-term dinner. Three cheers, indeed; but there was more to come, an unguessed epilogue, an encore played to a tragic audience.

3

It was a small but very comfortable and sunny room that Mrs. Wickett let to him. The house itself was ugly and pretentious; but that didn't matter. It was convenient--that was the main thing. For he liked, if the weather were mild enough, to stroll across to the playing fields in an afternoon and watch the games. He liked to smile and exchange a few words with the boys when they touched their caps to him. He made a special point of getting to know all the new boys and having them to tea with him during their first term. He always ordered a walnut cake with pink icing from Reddaway's, in the village, and during the winter term there were crumpets, too--a little pile of them in front of the fire, soaked in butter so that the bottom one lay in a little shallow pool. His guests found it fun to watch him make tea--mixing careful spoonfuls from different caddies. And he would ask the new boys where they lived, and if they had family connections at Brookfield. He kept watch to see that their plates were never empty, and punctually at five, after the session had lasted an hour, he would glance at the clock and say: "Well--umph--it's been very delightful--umph--meeting you like this--I'm sorry--umph--you can't stay. . . ." And he would smile and shake hands with them in the porch, leaving them to race across the road to the School with their comments. "Decent old boy, Chips. Gives you a jolly good tea, anyhow, and you *do* know when he wants you to push off. . . ."

And Chips also would be making his comments--to Mrs. Wickett when she entered his room to clear away the remains of the party. "A most--umph--interesting time, Mrs. Wickett. Young Branksome tells me--umph--that his uncle was Major Collingwood--the Collingwood we had here in--umph--nought-two, I think it was. Dear me, I remember Collingwood very well. I once thrashed him--umph--for climbing on to the gymnasium roof--to get a ball out of the gutter. Might have--

umph--broken his neck, the young fool. Do you remember him, Mrs. Wickett? He must have been in your time."

Mrs. Wickett, before she saved money, had been in charge of the linen room at the School.

"Yes, I knew 'im, sir. Cheeky, 'e was to me, gener'ly. But we never 'ad no bad words between us. Just cheeky-like. 'E never meant no harm. That kind never does, sir. Wasn't it 'im that got the medal, sir?"

"Yes, a D.S.O."

"Will you be wanting anything else, sir?"

"Nothing more now--umph--till chapel time. He was killed--in Egypt, I think. . . . Yes--umph--you can bring my supper about then."

"Very good, sir."

A pleasant, placid life, at Mrs. Wickett's. He had no worries; his pension was adequate, and there was a little money saved up besides. He could afford everything and anything he wanted. His room was furnished simply and with schoolmasterly taste: a few bookshelves and sporting trophies; a mantelpiece crowded with fixture cards and signed photographs of boys and men; a worn Turkey carpet; big easy-chairs; pictures on the wall of the Acropolis and the Forum. Nearly everything had come out of his old housemaster's room in School House. The books were chiefly classical, the classics having been his subject; there was, however, a seasoning of history and belles-lettres. There was also a bottom shelf piled up with cheap editions of detective novels. Chips enjoyed these. Sometimes he took down Vergil or Xenophon and read for a few moments, but he was soon back again with Doctor Thorndyke or Inspector French. He was not, despite his long years of assiduous teaching, a very profound classical scholar; indeed, he thought of Latin and Greek far more as dead languages from which English gentlemen ought to know a few quotations than as living tongues that had ever been spoken by living people. He liked those short leading articles in the *Times* that introduced a few tags that he recognized. To be among the dwindling number of people who understood such things was to him a kind of secret and valued freemasonry; it represented, he felt, one of the chief benefits to be derived from a classical education.

So there he lived, at Mrs. Wickett's, with his quiet enjoyments of reading and talking and remembering; an old man, white-haired and only a little bald, still fairly active for his years, drinking tea, receiving callers, busying himself with corrections for the next edition of the Brookfeldian Directory, writing his occasional letters in thin, spidery, but very legible script. He had new masters to tea, as well as new boys.

There were two of them that autumn term, and as they were leaving after their visit one of them commented: "Quite a character, the old boy, isn't he? All that fuss about mixing the tea--a typical bachelor, if ever there was one."

Which was oddly incorrect; because Chips was not a bachelor at all. He had married, though it was so long ago that none of the staff at Brookfield could remember his wife.

4

There came to him, stirred by the warmth of the fire and the gentle aroma of tea, a thousand tangled recollections of old times. Spring--the spring of 1896. He was forty-eight--an age at which a permanence of habits begins to be predictable. He had just been appointed housemaster; with this and his classical forms, he had made for himself a warm and busy corner of life. During the summer vacation he went up to the Lake District with Rowden, a colleague; they walked and climbed for a week, until Rowden had to leave suddenly on some family business. Chips stayed on alone at Wasdale Head, where he boarded in a small farmhouse.

One day, climbing on Great Gable, he noticed a girl waving excitedly from a dangerous-looking ledge. Thinking she was in difficulties, he hastened toward her, but in doing so slipped himself and wrenched his ankle. As it turned out, she was not in difficulties at all, but was merely signaling to a friend farther down the mountain; she was an expert climber, better even than Chips, who was pretty good. Thus he found himself the rescued instead of the rescuer; and neither role was one for which he had much relish. For he did not, he would have said, care for women; he never felt at home or at ease with them; and that monstrous creature beginning to be talked about, the New Woman of the nineties, filled him with horror. He was a quiet, conventional person, and the world, viewed from the haven of Brookfield, seemed to him full of distasteful innovations; there was a fellow named Bernard Shaw who had the strangest and most reprehensible opinions; there was Ibsen, too, with his disturbing plays; and there was this new craze for bicycling which was being taken up by women equally with men. Chips did not hold with all this modern newness and freedom. He had a vague notion, if he ever formulated it, that nice women were weak, timid, and delicate, and that nice men treated them with a polite but rather distant chivalry. He had not, therefore, expected to find a woman on Great Gable; but, having encountered one who seemed to need masculine help, it was even more terrifying that she should turn the tables by helping him. For she did. She and her friend had to. He could scarcely walk, and it was a hard job getting him down the steep track to Wasdale.

Her name was Katherine Bridges; she was twenty-five--young enough to be Chips's daughter. She had blue, flashing eyes and freckled cheeks and smooth straw-colored hair. She too was staying at a farm, on holiday with a girl friend, and as she considered herself responsible for Chips's accident, she used to bicycle along the side of the lake to the house in which the quiet, middle-aged, serious-looking man lay resting.

That was how she thought of him at first. And he, because she rode a bicycle and was unafraid to visit a man alone in a farmhouse sitting room, wondered vaguely what the world was coming to. His sprain put him at her mercy, and it was soon revealed to him how much he might need that mercy. She was a governess out of a job, with a little money saved up; she read and admired Ibsen; she believed that women ought to be admitted to the universities; she even thought they ought to have a vote. In politics she was a radical, with leanings toward the views of people like Bernard Shaw and William Morris. All her ideas and opinions she poured out to Chips during those summer afternoons at Wasdale Head; and he, because he was not very articulate, did not at first think it worth while to contradict them. Her friend went away, but she stayed; what *could* you do with such a person, Chips thought. He used to hobble with sticks along a footpath leading to the tiny church; there was a stone slab on the wall, and it was comfortable to sit down, facing the sunlight and the green-brown majesty of the Gable and listening to the chatter of--well, yes, Chips had to admit it--a very beautiful girl.

He had never met anyone like her. He had always thought that the modern type, this "new woman" business, would repel him; and here she was, making him positively look forward to the glimpse of her safety bicycle careering along the lakeside road. And she, too, had never met anyone like *him*. She had always thought that middle-aged men who read the *Times* and disapproved of modernity were terrible bores; yet here he was, claiming her interest and attention far more than youths of her own age. She liked him, initially, because he was so hard to get to know, because he had gentle and quiet manners, because his opinions dated from those utterly impossible seventies and eighties and even earlier--yet were, for all that, so thoroughly honest; and be-cause--because his eyes were brown and he looked charming when he smiled. "Of course, *I* shall call you Chips, too," she said, when she learned that was his nickname at school.

Within a week they were head over heels in love; before Chips could walk without a stick, they considered themselves engaged; and they were married in London a week before the beginning of the au-tumn term.

5

When Chips, dreaming through the hours at Mrs. Wickett's, recollected those days, he used to look down at his feet and wonder which one it was that had performed so signal a service. That, the trivial cause of so many momentous happenings, was the one thing of which details evaded him. But he resaw the glorious hump of the Gable (he had never visited the Lake District since), and the mouse-gray depths of Wastwater under the Screes; he could resmell the washed air after heavy rain, and refollow the ribbon of the pass across to Sty Head. So clearly it lingered, that time of dizzy happiness, those evening strolls by the waterside, her cool voice and her gay laughter. She had been a very happy person, always.

They had both been so eager, planning a future together; but he had been rather serious about it, even a little awed. It would be all right, of course, her coming to Brookfield; other housemasters were married. And she liked boys, she told him, and would enjoy living among them. "Oh, Chips, I'm so glad you are what you are. I was afraid you were a solicitor or a stockbroker or a dentist or a man with a big cotton business in Manchester. When I first met you, I mean. Schoolmastering's so different, so important, don't you think? To be influencing those who are going to grow up and matter to the world . . ."

Chips said he hadn't thought of it like that--or, at least, not often. He did his best; that was all anyone could do in any job.

"Yes, of course, Chips. I do love you for saying simple things like that."

And one morning--another memory gem-clear when he turned to it--he had for some reason been afflicted with an acute desire to depreciate himself and all his attainments. He had told her of his only mediocre degree, of his occasional difficulties of discipline, of the certainty that he would never get a promotion, and of his complete ineligibility to marry a young and ambitious girl. And at the end of it all she had laughed in answer.

She had no parents and was married from the house of an aunt in Ealing. On the night before the wedding, when Chips left the house to return to his hotel, she said, with mock gravity: "This is an occasion, you know--this last farewell of ours. I feel rather like a new boy beginning his first term with you. Not scared, mind you--but just, for once, in a thoroughly respectful mood. Shall I call you 'sir'--or would 'Mr. Chips' be the right thing? 'Mr. Chips,' I think. Good-bye, then--good-bye, Mr. Chips. . . ."

(A hansom clop-clopping in the roadway; green-pale gas lamps flickering on a wet pavement; newsboys shouting something about South Africa; Sherlock Holmes in Baker Street.)

"Good-bye, Mr. Chips. . . ."

6

There had followed then a time of such happiness that Chips, remembering it long afterward, hardly believed it could ever have happened before or since in the world. For his marriage was a triumphant success. Katherine conquered Brookfield as she had conquered Chips; she was immensely popular with boys and masters alike. Even the wives of the masters, tempted at first to be jealous of one so young and lovely, could not long resist her charms.

But most remarkable of all was the change she made in Chips. Till his marriage he had been a dry and rather neutral sort of person; liked and thought well of by Brookfield in general, but not of the stuff that makes for great popularity or that stirs great affection. He had been at Brookfield for over a quarter of a century, long enough to have established himself as a decent fellow and a hard worker; but just too long for anyone to believe him capable of ever being much more. He had, in fact, already begun to sink into that creeping dry rot of pedagogy which is the worst and ultimate pitfall of the profession; giving the same lessons year after year had formed a groove into which the other affairs of his life adjusted themselves with insidious ease. He worked well; he was conscientious; he was a fixture that gave service, satisfaction, confidence, everything except inspiration.

And then came this astonishing girl-wife whom nobody had expected--least of all Chips himself. She made him, to all appearances, a new man; though most of the newness was really a warming to life of things that were old, imprisoned, and unguessed. His eyes gained sparkle; his mind, which was adequately if not brilliantly equipped, began to move more adventurously. The one thing he had always had, a sense of humor, blossomed into a sudden richness to which his years lent maturity. He began to feel a greater sureness; his discipline improved to a point at which it could become, in a sense, less rigid; he became more popular. When he had first come to Brookfield he had aimed to be loved, honored, and obeyed--but obeyed, at any rate. Obedience he had secured, and honor had been granted him; but only now came love, the sudden love of boys for a man who was kind without being soft, who understood them well enough, but not too much, and whose private happiness linked them with their own. He began to make little jokes, the sort that schoolboys like--mnemonics and puns that raised laughs and at the same time imprinted something in the mind. There was one that never failed to please, though it was only a sample of many others. Whenever his Roman History forms came to deal with the Lex Canuleia, the law that permitted patricians to marry plebeians, Chips used to add: "So that, you see, if Miss Plebs wanted Mr. Patrician to marry her, and he said he couldn't, she probably replied: 'Oh yes, you can, you liar!'" Roars of laughter.

And Kathie broadened his views and opinions, also, giving him an outlook far beyond the roofs and turrets of Brookfield, so that he saw his country as something deep and gracious to which Brookfield was but one of many feeding streams. She had a cleverer brain than his, and he could not confuse her ideas even if and when he disagreed with them; he remained, for instance, a Conservative in politics, despite all her radical-socialist talk. But even where he did not accept, he absorbed; her young idealism worked upon his maturity to produce an amalgam very gentle and wise.

Sometimes she persuaded him completely. Brookfield, for example, ran a mission in East London, to which boys and parents contributed generously with money but rarely with personal contact. It was Katherine who suggested that a team from the mission should come up to Brookfield and play one of the School's elevens at soccer. The idea was so revolutionary that from anyone but Katherine it could not have survived its first frosty reception. To introduce a group of slum boys to the serene pleasaunces of better-class youngsters seemed at first a wanton stirring of all kinds of things that had better be left untouched. The whole staff was against it, and the School, if its opinion could have been taken, was probably against it too. Everyone was certain that the East End lads would be hooligans, or else that they would be made to feel uncomfortable; anyhow, there would be "incidents," and everyone would be confused and upset. Yet Katherine persisted.

"Chips," she said, "they're wrong, you know, and I'm right. I'm looking ahead to the future, they and you are looking back to the past. England isn't always going to be divided into officers and 'other ranks.'

And those Poplar boys are just as important--to England--as Brookfield is. You've got to have them here, Chips. You can't satisfy your conscience by writing a check for a few guineas and keeping them at arm's length. Besides, they're proud of Brookfield--just as you are. Years hence, maybe, boys of that sort will be coming here--a few of them, at any rate. Why not? Why ever not? Chips, dear, remember this is eighteen-ninety-seven--not sixty-seven, when you were up at Cambridge. You got your ideas well stuck in those days, and good ideas they were too, a lot of them. But a few--just a few, Chips--want unsticking. . . ."

Rather to her surprise, he gave way and suddenly became a keen advocate of the proposal, and the *volte-face* was so complete that the authorities were taken unawares and found themselves consenting to the dangerous experiment. The boys from Poplar arrived at Brookfield one Saturday afternoon, played soccer with the School's second team, were honorably defeated by seven goals to five, and later had high tea with the School team in the Dining Hall. They then met the Head and were shown over the School, and Chips saw them off at the railway station in the evening. Everything had passed without the slightest hitch of any kind, and it was clear that the visitors were taking away with them as fine an impression as they had left behind.

They took back with them also the memory of a charming woman who had met them and talked to them; for once, years later, during the War, a private stationed at a big military camp near Brookfield called on Chips and said he had been one of that first visiting team. Chips gave him tea and chatted with him, till at length, shaking hands, the man said: "And 'ow's the missus, sir? I remember her very well."

"Do you?" Chips answered, eagerly. "Do you remember her?"

"Rather. I should think anyone would."

And Chips replied: "They don't, you know. At least, not here. Boys come and go; new faces all the time; memories don't last. Even masters don't stay forever. Since last year--when old Gribble retired--he's--um--the School butler--there hasn't been anyone here who ever saw my wife. She died, you know, less than a year after your visit. In ninety-eight."

"I'm real sorry to 'ear that, sir. There's two or three o' my pals, anyhow, who remember 'er clear as anything, though we did only see 'er that wunst. Yes, we remember 'er, all right."

"I'm very glad. . . . That was a grand day we all had--and a fine game, too."

18

"One o' the best days aht I ever 'ad in me life. Wish it was then and not nah--straight, I do. I'm off to Frawnce to-morrer."

A month or so later Chips heard that he had been killed at Passchendaele.

7

And so it stood, a warm and vivid patch in his life, casting a radiance that glowed in a thousand recollections. Twilight at Mrs. Wickett's, when the School bell clanged for call-over, brought them back to him in a cloud--Katherine scampering along the stone corridors, laughing beside him at some "howler" in an essay he was marking, taking the cello part in a Mozart trio for the School concert, her creamy arm sweeping over the brown sheen of the instrument. She had been a good player and a fine musician. And Katherine furred and muffed for the December house matches, Katherine at the Garden Party that followed Speech Day Prize-giving, Katherine tendering her advice in any little problem that arose. Good advice, too--which he did not always take, but which always influenced him.

"Chips, dear, I'd let them off if I were you. After all, it's nothing very serious."

"I know. I'd like to let them off, but if I do I'm afraid they'll do it again."

"Try telling them that, frankly, and give them the chance."

"I might."

And there were other things, occasionally, that *were* serious.

"You know, Chips, having all these hundreds of boys cooped up here is really an unnatural arrangement, when you come to think about it. So that when anything does occur that oughtn't to, don't you think it's a bit unfair to come down on them as if it were their own fault for being here?"

"Don't know about that, Kathie, but I do know that for everybody's sake we have to be pretty strict about this sort of thing. One black sheep can contaminate others."

"After he himself has been contaminated to begin with. After all, that's what probably *did* happen, isn't it?"

"Maybe. We can't help it. Anyhow, I believe Brookfield is better than a lot of other schools. All the more reason to keep it so."

"But this boy, Chips . . . you're going to sack him?"

"The Head probably will, when I tell him."

"And you're going to tell the Head?"

"It's a duty, I'm afraid."

"Couldn't you think about it a bit . . . talk to the boy again . . . find out how it began. . . . After all--apart from this business--isn't he rather a nice boy?"

"Oh, he's all right."

"Then, Chips dear, don't you think there *ought* to be some other way. . . ."

And so on. About once in ten times he was adamant and wouldn't be persuaded. In about half of these exceptional cases he afterward rather wished he had taken her advice. And years later, whenever he had trouble with a boy, he was always at the mercy of a softening wave of reminiscence; the boy would stand there, waiting to be told his punishment, and would see, if he were observant, the brown eyes twinkle into a shine that told him all was well. But he did not guess that at such a moment Chips was remembering something that had happened long before he was born; that Chips was thinking: Young ruffian, I'm hanged if *I* can think of any reason to let him off, but I'll bet *she* would have done!

But she had not always pleaded for leniency. On rather rare occasions she urged severity where Chips was inclined to be forgiving. "I don't like his type, Chips. He's too cocksure of himself. If he's looking for trouble I should certainly let him have it."

What a host of little incidents, all deep-buried in the past--problems that had once been urgent, arguments that had once been keen, anecdotes that were funny only because one remembered the fun. Did any emotion really matter when the last trace of it had vanished from human memory; and if that were so, what a crowd of emotions clung to him as to their last home before annihilation! He must be kind to them, must treasure them in his mind before their long sleep. That affair of Archer's resignation, for instance--a queer business, that was. And that affair about the rat that Dunster put in the organ loft while old Ogilvie was taking choir practice. Ogilvie was dead and Dunster drowned at Jutland; of others who had witnessed or heard of the incident, probably most had forgotten. And it had been like that, with other incidents, for centuries. He had a sudden vision of thousands and thousands of boys, from the age of Elizabeth onward; dynasty upon dynasty of masters;

long epochs of Brookfield history that had left not even a ghostly record. Who knew why the old fifth-form room was called "the Pit"? There was probably a reason, to begin with; but it had since been lost-- lost like the lost books of Livy. And what happened at Brookfield when Cromwell fought at Naseby, near by? How did Brookfield react to the great scare of the "Forty-Five"? Was there a whole holiday when news came of Waterloo? And so on, up to the earliest time that he himself could remember--1870, and Wetherby saying, by way of small talk after their first and only interview: "Looks as if we shall have to settle with the Prussians ourselves one of these fine days, eh?"

When Chips remembered things like this he often felt that he would write them down and make a book of them; and during his years at Mrs. Wickett's he sometimes went even so far as to make desultory notes in an exercise book. But he was soon brought up against difficulties--the chief one being that writing tired him, both mentally and physically. Somehow, too, his recollections lost much of their flavor when they were written down; that story about Rushton and the sack of potatoes, for instance--it would seem quite tame in print, but Lord, how funny it had been at the time! It was funny, too, to remember it; though perhaps if you didn't remember Rushton . . . and who would, anyway, after all those years? It was such a long time ago. . . . Mrs. Wickett, did you ever know a fellow named Rushton? Before your time, I dare say . . . went to Burma in some government job . . . or was it Borneo? . . . Very funny fellow, Rushton. . . . And there he was, dreaming again before the fire, dreaming of times and incidents in which he alone could take secret interest. Funny and sad, comic and tragic, they all mixed up in his mind, and some day, however hard it proved, he *would* sort them out and make a book of them. . . .

8

And there was always in his mind that spring day in ninety-eight when he had paced through Brookfield village as in some horrifying nightmare, half struggling to escape into an outside world where the sun still shone and where everything had happened differently. Young Faulkner had met him there in the lane outside the School. "Please, sir, may I have the afternoon off? My people are coming up."

"Eh? What's that? Oh yes, yes. . . ."

"Can I miss Chapel, too, sir?"

"Yes . . . yes . . ."

"And may I go to the station to meet them?"

He nearly answered: "You can go to blazes for all I care. My wife is dead and my child is dead, and I wish I were dead myself."

Actually he nodded and stumbled on. He did not want to talk to anybody or to receive condolences; he wanted to get used to things, if he could, before facing the kind words of others. He took his fourth form as usual after call-over, setting them grammar to learn by heart while he himself stayed at his desk in a cold, continuing trance. Suddenly someone said: "Please, sir, there are a lot of letters for you."

So there were; he had been leaning his elbows on them; they were all addressed to him by name. He tore them open one after the other, but each contained nothing but a blank sheet of paper. He thought in a distant way that it was rather peculiar, but he made no comment; the incident gave hardly an impact upon his vastly greater preoccupations. Not till days afterward did he realize that it had been a piece of April foolery.

They had died on the same day, the mother and the child just born; on April 1, 1898.

9

Chips changed his more commodious apartments in School House for his old original bachelor quarters. He thought at first he would give up his housemastership, but the Head persuaded him otherwise; and later he was glad. The work gave him something to do, filled up an emptiness in his mind and heart. He was different; everyone noticed it. Just as marriage had added something, so did bereavement; after the first stupor of grief he became suddenly the kind of man whom boys, at any rate, unhesitatingly classed as "old." It was not that he was less active; he could still knock up a half century on the cricket field; nor was it that he had lost any interest or keenness in his work. Actually, too, his hair had been graying for years; yet now, for the first time, people seemed to notice it. He was fifty. Once, after some energetic fives, during which he had played as well as many a fellow half his age, he overheard a boy saying: "Not half bad for an old chap like him."

Chips, when he was over eighty, used to recount that incident with many chuckles. "Old at fifty, eh? Umph--it was Naylor who said that, and Naylor can't be far short of fifty himself by now! I wonder if he still thinks that fifty's such an age? Last I heard of him, he was lawyering, and lawyers live long--look at Halsbury--umph--Chancellor at eighty-two, and died at ninety-nine. There's an--umph--age for you! Too old at fifty--why, fellows like that are too *young* at fifty. . . . I was myself . . . a mere infant. . . ."

And there was a sense in which it was true. For with the new century there settled upon Chips a mellowness that gathered all his developing mannerisms and his oft-repeated jokes into a single harmony. No longer did he have those slight and occasional disciplinary troubles, or feel diffident about his own work and worth. He found that his pride in Brookfield reflected back, giving him cause for pride in himself and his position. It was a service that gave him freedom to be supremely and completely himself. He had won, by seniority and ripeness, an uncharted no-man's-land of privilege; he had acquired the right to those gentle eccentricities that so often attack schoolmasters and parsons. He wore his gown till it was almost too tattered to hold together; and when he stood on the wooden bench by Big Hall steps to take call-over, it was with an air of mystic abandonment to ritual. He held the School List, a long sheet curling over a board; and each boy, as he passed, spoke his own name for Chips to verify and then tick off on the list. That verifying glance was an easy and favorite subject of mimicry throughout the School--steel-rimmed spectacles slipping down the nose, eyebrows lifted, one a little higher than the other, a gaze half rapt, half quizzical. And on windy days, with gown and white hair and School List fluttering in uproarious confusion, the whole thing became a comic turn sandwiched between afternoon games and the return to classes.

Some of those names, in little snatches of a chorus, recurred to him ever afterward without any effort of memory. . . . Ainsworth, Attwood, Avonmore, Babcock, Baggs, Barnard, Bassenthwaite, Battersby, Beccles, Bedford-Marshall, Bentley, Best . . .

Another one:--

. . . Unsley, Vailes, Wadham, Wagstaff, Wallington, Waters Primus, Waters Secundus, Watling, Waveney, Webb . . .

And yet another that comprised, as he used to tell his fourth-form Latinists, an excellent example of a hexameter:--

. . . Lancaster, Latton, Lemare, Lytton-Bosworth, MacGonigall, Mansfield . . .

Where had they all gone to, he often pondered; those threads he had once held together, how far had they scattered, some to break, others to weave into unknown patterns? The strange randomness of the world beguiled him, that randomness which never would, so long as the world lasted, give meaning to those choruses again.

And behind Brookfield, as one may glimpse a mountain behind another mountain when the mist clears, he saw the world of change and conflict; and he saw it, more than he realized, with the remembered eyes of Kathie. She had not been able to bequeath him all her mind, still less the brilliance of it; but she had left him with a calmness and a poise that accorded well with his own inward emotions. It was typical of him that he did not share the general jingo bitterness against the Boers. Not that he was a pro-Boer--he was far too traditional for that, and he disliked the kind of people who *were* pro-Boers; but still, it did cross his mind at times that the Boers were engaged in a struggle that had a curious similarity to those of certain English history-book heroes--Hereward the Wake, for instance, or Caractacus. He once tried to shock his fifth form by suggesting this, but they only thought it was one of his little jokes.

However heretical he might be about the Boers, he was orthodox about Mr. Lloyd George and the famous Budget. He did not care for either of them. And when, years later, L. G. came as the guest of honor to a Brookfield Speech Day, Chips said, on being presented to him: "Mr. Lloyd George, I am nearly old enough--umph--to remember you as a young man, and--umph--I confess that you seem to me--umph--to have improved--umph--a great deal." The Head standing with them, was rather aghast; but L. G. laughed heartily and talked to Chips more than to anyone else during the ceremonial that followed.

"Just like Chips," was commented afterward. "He gets away with it. I suppose at that age anything you say to anybody is all right. . . ."

10

In 1900 old Meldrum, who had succeeded Wetherby as Head and had held office for three decades, died suddenly from pneumonia; and in the interval before the appointment of a successor, Chips became Acting Head of Brookfield. There was just the faintest chance that the Governors might make the appointment a permanent one; but Chips was not really disappointed when they brought in a youngster of thirty-seven, glittering with Firsts and Blues and with the kind of personality that could reduce Big Hall to silence by the mere lifting of an eyebrow. Chips was not in the running with that kind of person; he never had been and never would be, and he knew it. He was an altogether milder and less ferocious animal.

Those years before his retirement in 1913 were studded with sharply remembered pictures.

A May morning; the clang of the School bell at an unaccustomed time; everyone summoned to assemble in Big Hall. Ralston, the new Head, very pontifical and aware of himself, fixing the multitude with a cold, presaging severity. "You will all be deeply grieved to hear that His Majesty King Edward the Seventh died this morning. . . . There will be no school this afternoon, but a service will be held in the Chapel at four-thirty."

A summer morning on the railway line near Brookfield. The railwaymen were on strike, soldiers were driving the engines, stones had been thrown at trains. Brookfield boys were patrolling the line, thinking the whole business great fun. Chips, who was in charge, stood a little way off, talking to a man at the gate of a cottage. Young Cricklade approached. "Please, sir, what shall we do if we meet any strikers?"

"Would you like to meet one?"

"I--I don't know, sir."

God bless the boy--he talked of them as if they were queer animals out of a zoo! "Well, here you are, then--umph--you can meet Mr. Jones--he's a striker. When he's on duty he has charge of the signal box at the station. You've put your life in his hands many a time."

Afterward the story went round the School: There was Chips, talking to a striker. Talking to a striker. Might have been quite friendly, the way they were talking together.

Chips, thinking it over a good many times, always added to himself that Kathie would have approved, and would also have been amused.

Because always, whatever happened and however the avenues of politics twisted and curved, he had faith in England, in English flesh and blood, and in Brookfield as a place whose ultimate worth depended on whether she fitted herself into the English scene with dignity and without disproportion. He had been left a vision that grew clearer with each year--of an England for which days of ease were nearly over, of a nation steering into channels where a hair's breadth of error might be catastrophic. He remembered the Diamond Jubilee; there had been a whole holiday at Brookfield, and he had taken Kathie to London to see the procession. That old and legendary lady, sitting in her carriage like some crumbling wooden doll, had symbolized impressively so many things that, like herself, were nearing an end. Was it only the century, or was it an epoch?

And then that frenzied Edwardian decade, like an electric lamp that goes brighter and whiter just before it burns itself out.

Strikes and lockouts, champagne suppers and unemployed marchers, Chinese labor, tariff reform, *H.M.S. Dreadnought*, Marconi, Home Rule for Ireland, Doctor Crippen, suffragettes, the lines of Chatalja. . .
.

An April evening, windy and rainy; the fourth form construing Vergil, not very intelligently, for there was exciting news in the papers; young Grayson, in particular, was careless and preoccupied. A quiet, nervous boy.

"Grayson, stay behind--umph--after the rest."

Then:--

"Grayson, I don't want to be--umph--severe, because you are generally pretty good--umph--in your work, but to-day--you don't seem--umph--to have been trying at all. Is anything the matter?"

"N-no, sir."

"Well--umph--we'll say no more about it, but--umph--I shall expect better things next time."

Next morning it was noised around the School that Grayson's father had sailed on the *Titanic,* and that no news had yet come through as to his fate.

Grayson was excused lessons; for a whole day the School centred emotionally upon his anxieties. Then came news that his father had been among those rescued.

Chips shook hands with the boy. "Well, umph--I'm delighted, Grayson. A happy ending. You must be feeling pretty pleased with life."

"Y-yes, sir."

A quiet, nervous boy. And it was Grayson Senior, not Junior, with whom Chips was destined later to condole.

11

And then the row with Ralston. Funny thing, Chips had never liked him; he was efficient, ruthless, ambitious, but not, somehow, very likable. He had, admittedly, raised the status of Brookfield as a school, and for the first time in memory there was a longish waiting list. Ralston was a live wire; a fine power transmitter, but you had to beware of him.

Chips had never bothered to beware of him; he was not attracted by the man, but he served him willingly enough and quite loyally. Or, rather, he served Brookfield. He knew that Ralston did not like him, either; but that didn't seem to matter. He felt himself sufficiently protected by age and seniority from the fate of other masters whom Ralston had failed to like.

Then suddenly, in 1908, when he had just turned sixty, came Ralston's urbane ultimatum. "Mr. Chipping, have you ever thought you would like to retire?"

Chips stared about him in that book-lined study, startled by the question, wondering why Ralston should have asked it. He said, at length: "No--umph--I can't say that--umph--I have thought much about it--umph--yet."

"Well, Mr. Chipping, the suggestion is there for you to consider. The Governors would, of course, agree to your being adequately pensioned."

Abruptly Chips flamed up. "But--umph--I don't want--to retire. I don't--umph--need to consider it."

"Nevertheless, I suggest that you do."

"But--umph--I don't see--why--I should!"

"In that case, things are going to be a little difficult."

"Difficult? Why--difficult?"

And then they set to, Ralston getting cooler and harder, Chips getting warmer and more passionate, till at last Ralston said, icily: "Since you force me to use plain words, Mr. Chipping, you shall have them. For some time past, you haven't been pulling your weight here. Your methods of teaching are slack and old-fashioned; your personal habits are slovenly; and you ignore my instructions in a way which, in a younger man, I should regard as rank insubordination. It won't do, Mr. Chipping, and you must ascribe it to my forbearance that I have put up with it so long."

"But--" Chips began, in sheer bewilderment; and then he took up isolated words out of that extraordinary indictment. *"Slovenly--umph--you said--?"*

"Yes, look at the gown you're wearing. I happen to know that that gown of yours is a subject of continual amusement throughout the School."

Chips knew it, too, but it had never seemed to him a very regrettable matter.

He went on: "And--you also said--umph--something about--*insubordination--?"*

"No, I didn't. I said that in a younger man I should have regarded it as that. In your case it's probably a mixture of slackness and obstinacy. This question of Latin pronunciation, for instance--I think I told you years ago that I wanted the new style used throughout the School. The other masters obeyed me; you prefer to stick to your old methods, and the result is simply chaos and inefficiency."

At last Chips had something tangible that he could tackle. "Oh, *that!"* he answered, scornfully. "Well, I--umph--I admit that I don't agree with the new pronunciation. I never did. Umph--a lot of nonsense, in my opinion. Making boys say 'Kickero' at school when--umph--for the rest of their lives they'll say 'Cicero'--if they ever--umph--say it at all. And instead of 'vicissim'--God bless my soul--you'd make them say, 'We kiss 'im'! Umph--umph!" And he chuckled momentarily, forgetting that he was in Ralston's study and not in his own friendly form room.

"Well, there you are, Mr. Chipping--that's just an example of what I complain of. You hold one opinion and I hold another, and, since you decline to give way, there can't very well be any alternative. I aim to make Brookfield a thoroughly up-to-date school. I'm a science man myself, but for all that I have no objection to the classics--provided that they are taught efficiently. Because they are dead languages is no reason why they should be dealt with in a dead educational technique.

I understand, Mr. Chipping, that your Latin and Greek lessons are exactly the same as they were when I began here ten years ago?"

Chips answered, slowly and with pride: "For that matter--umph--they are the same as when your predecessor--Mr. Meldrum--came here, and that--umph--was thirty-eight years ago. We began here, Mr. Meldrum and I--in--umph--in 1870. And it was--um--Mr. Meldrum's predecessor, Mr. Wetherby--who first approved my syllabus. 'You'll take the Cicero for the fourth,' he said to me. Cicero, too--not Kickero!"

"Very interesting, Mr. Chipping, but once again it proves my point--you live too much in the past, and not enough in the present and future. Times are changing, whether you realize it or not. Modern parents are beginning to demand something more for their three years' school fees than a few scraps of languages that nobody speaks. Besides, your boys don't learn even what they're supposed to learn. None of them last year got through the Lower Certificate."

And suddenly, in a torrent of thoughts too pressing to be put into words, Chips made answer to himself. These examinations and certificates and so on--what did they matter? And all this efficiency and up-to-dateness--what did *that* matter, either? Ralston was trying to run Brookfield like a factory--a factory for turning out a snob culture based on money and machines. The old gentlemanly traditions of family and broad acres were changing, as doubtless they were bound to; but instead of widening them to form a genuine inclusive democracy of duke and dustman, Ralston was narrowing them upon the single issue of a fat banking account. There never had been so many rich men's sons at Brookfield. The Speech Day Garden Party was like Ascot. Ralston met these wealthy fellows in London clubs and persuaded them that Brookfield was *the* coming school, and, since they couldn't buy their way into Eton or Harrow, they greedily swallowed the bait. Awful fellows, some of them--though others were decent enough. Financiers, company promoters, pill manufacturers. One of them gave his son five pounds a week pocket money. Vulgar . . . ostentatious . . . all the hectic rotten-ripeness of the age. . . . And once Chips had got into trouble because of some joke he had made about the name and ancestry of a boy named Isaacstein. The boy wrote home about it, and Isaacstein *père* sent an angry letter to Ralston. Touchy, no sense of humor, no sense of proportion--that was the matter with them, these new fellows. . . . No sense of proportion. And it was a sense of proportion, above all things, that Brookfield ought to teach--not so much Latin or Greek or Chemistry or Mechanics. And you couldn't expect to

test that sense of proportion by setting papers and granting certificates.
. . .

All this flashed through his mind in an instant of protest and indignation, but he did not say a word of it. He merely gathered his tattered gown together and with an "umph--umph" walked a few paces away. He had had enough of the argument. At the door he turned and said: "I don't--umph--intend to resign--and you can--umph--do what you like about it!"

Looking back upon that scene in the calm perspective of a quarter of a century, Chips could find it in his heart to feel a little sorry for Ralston. Particularly when, as it happened, Ralston had been in such complete ignorance of the forces he was dealing with. So, for that matter, had Chips himself. Neither had correctly estimated the toughness of Brookfield tradition, and its readiness to defend itself and its defenders. For it had so chanced that a small boy, waiting to see Ralston that morning, had been listening outside the door during the whole of the interview; he had been thrilled by it, naturally, and had told his friends. Some of these, in a surprisingly short time, had told their parents; so that very soon it was common knowledge that Ralston had insulted Chips and had demanded his resignation. The amazing result was a spontaneous outburst of sympathy and partisanship such as Chips, in his wildest dreams, had never envisaged. He found, rather to his astonishment, that Ralston was thoroughly unpopular; he was feared and respected, but not liked; and in this issue of Chips the dislike rose to a point where it conquered fear and demolished even respect. There was talk of having some kind of public riot in the School if Ralston succeeded in banishing Chips. The masters, many of them young men who agreed that Chips was hopelessly old-fashioned, rallied round him nevertheless because they hated Ralston's slave driving and saw in the old veteran a likely champion. And one day the Chairman of the Governors, Sir John Rivers, visited Brookfield, ignored Ralston, and went direct to Chips. "A fine fellow, Rivers," Chips would say, telling the story to Mrs. Wickett for the dozenth time. "Not--umph--a very brilliant boy in class. I remember he could never--umph--master his verbs. And now--umph--I see in the papers--they've made him--umph--a baronet. It just shows you--umph--it just shows you."

Sir John had said, on that morning in 1908, taking Chips by the arm as they walked round the deserted cricket pitches: "Chips, old boy, I hear you've been having the deuce of a row with Ralston. Sorry to hear about it, for your sake--but I want you to know that the Governors are with you to a man. We don't like the fellow a great deal. Very clever and all that, but a bit too clever, if you ask me. Claims to have doubled the School's endowment funds by some monkeying on the Stock Exchange. Dare say he has, but a chap like that wants watching. So if he starts chucking his weight about with you, tell him very politely he can go to the devil. The Governors don't want you to resign. Brookfield wouldn't be the same without you, and they know it. We all know it. You can stay here till you're a hundred if you feel like it--indeed, it's our hope that you will."

And at that--both then and often when he recounted it afterward--Chips broke down.

12

So he stayed on at Brookfield, having as little to do with Ralston as possible. And in 1911 Ralston left, "to better himself"; he was offered the headship of one of the greater public schools. His successor was a man named Chatteris, whom Chips liked; he was even younger than Ralston had been--thirty-four. He was supposed to be very brilliant; at any rate, he was modern (Natural Sciences Tripos), friendly, and sympathetic. Recognizing in Chips a Brookfield institution, he courteously and wisely accepted the situation.

In 1913 Chips had had bronchitis and was off duty for nearly the whole of the winter term. It was that which made him decide to resign that summer, when he was sixty-five. After all, it was a good, ripe age; and Ralston's straight words had, in some ways, had an effect. He felt that it would not be fair to hang on if he could not decently do his job. Besides, he would not sever himself completely. He would take rooms across the road, with the excellent Mrs. Wickett who had once been linen-room maid; he could visit the School whenever he wanted, and could still, in a sense, remain a part of it.

At that final end-of-term dinner, in July 1913, Chips received his farewell presentations and made a speech. It was not a very long speech, but it had a good many jokes in it, and was made twice as long, perhaps, by the laughter that impeded its progress. There were several Latin quotations in it, as well as a reference to the Captain of the School, who, Chips said, had been guilty of exaggeration in speaking of his (Chips's) services to Brookfield. "But then--umph--he comes of an--umph--exaggerating family. I--um--remember--once--having to thrash his father--for it. [Laughter] I gave him one mark--umph--for a Latin translation, and he--umph--exaggerated the one into a seven! Umph--umph!" Roars of laughter and tumultuous cheers! A typical Chips remark, everyone thought.

And then he mentioned that he had been at Brookfield for forty-two years, and that he had been very happy there. "It has been my life," he said, simply. *"O mihi praeteritos referat si Jupiter annos. . . .* Umph--I need not--of course--translate. . . ." Much laughter. "I remember lots of changes at Brookfield. I remember the--um--the first bicycle. I remember when there was no gas or electric light and we used to have a member of the domestic staff called a lamp-boy--he did nothing else but clean and trim and light lamps throughout the School. I remember when there was a hard frost that lasted for seven weeks in the winter term--there were no games, and the whole School learned to skate on the fens. Eighteen-eighty-something, that was. I remember when two-thirds of the School went down with German measles and Big Hall was turned into a hospital ward. I remember the great bonfire we had on Mafeking night. It was lit too near the pavilion and we had to send for the fire brigade to put it out. And the firemen were having their own celebrations and most of them were--um--in a regrettable condition. [Laughter] I remember Mrs. Brool, whose photograph is still in the tuckshop; she served there until an uncle in Australia left her a lot of money. In fact, I remember so much that I often think I ought to write a book. Now what should I call it? 'Memories of Rod and Lines'--eh? [Cheers and laughter. That was a good one, people thought--one of Chips's best.] Well, well, perhaps I shall write it, some day. But I'd rather tell you about it, really. I remember . . . I remember . . . but chiefly I remember all your faces. I never forget them. I have thousands of faces in my mind--the faces of boys. If you come and see me again in years to come--as I hope you all will--I shall try to remember those older faces of yours, but it's just possible I shan't be able to--and then some day you'll see me somewhere and I shan't recognize you and you'll say to yourself, 'The old boy doesn't remember me.' [Laughter] But I *do* remember you--as you are *now*. That's the point. In my mind you never grow up at all. Never. Sometimes, for instance, when people talk to me about our respected Chairman of the Governors, I think to myself, 'Ah, yes, a jolly little chap with hair that sticks up on top--and absolutely no idea whatever about the difference between a Gerund and a Gerundive.' [Loud laughter] Well, well, I mustn't go on--umph--all night. Think of me sometimes as I shall certainly think of you. *Haec olim meminisse juvabit . . .* again I need not translate." Much laughter and shouting and prolonged cheers.

August 1913. Chips went for a cure to Wiesbaden, where he lodged at the home of the German master at Brookfield, Herr Staefel, with whom he had become friendly. Staefel was thirty years his junior, but the two men got on excellently. In September, when term began, Chips returned and took up residence at Mrs. Wickett's. He felt a great deal stronger and fitter after his holiday, and almost wished he had not retired. Nevertheless, he found plenty to do. He had all the new boys to tea. He watched all the important matches on the Brookfield ground. Once a term he dined with the Head, and once also with the masters. He took on the preparation and editing of a new Brookfeldian Directory. He accepted presidency of the Old Boys' Club and went to dinners in London. He wrote occasional articles, full of jokes and Latin quotations, for the Brookfield terminal magazine. He read his *Times* every morning--very thoroughly; and he also began to read detective stories--he had been keen on them ever since the first thrills of Sherlock. Yes, he was quite busy, and quite happy, too. A year later, in 1914, he again attended the end-of-term dinner. There was a lot of war talk--civil war in Ulster, and trouble between Austria and Serbia. Herr Staefel, who was leaving for Germany the next day, told Chips he thought the Balkan business wouldn't come to anything.

13

The War years.

The first shock, and then the first optimism. The Battle of the Marne, the Russian steam-roller, Kitchener.

"Do you think it will last long, sir?"

Chips, questioned as he watched the first trial game of the season, gave quite a cheery answer. He was, like thousands of others, hopelessly wrong; but, unlike thousands of others, he did not afterward conceal the fact. "We ought to have--um--finished it--um--by Christmas. The Germans are already beaten. But why? Are you thinking of--um--joining up, Forrester?"

Joke--because Forrester was the smallest new boy Brookfield had ever had--about four feet high above his muddy football boots. (But not so much a joke, when you came to think of it afterward; for he was killed in 1918--shot down in flames over Cambrai.) But one didn't guess what lay ahead. It seemed tragically sensational when the first Old Brookfeldian was killed in action--in September. Chips thought, when that news came: A hundred years ago boys from this school were fighting *against* the French. Strange, in a way, that the sacrifices of one generation should so cancel out those of another. He tried to express this to Blades, the Head of School House; but Blades, eighteen years old and already in training for a cadetship, only laughed. What had all that history stuff to do with it, anyhow? Just old Chips with one of his queer ideas, that's all.

1915. Armies clenched in deadlock from the sea to Switzerland. The Dardanelles. Gallipoli. Military camps springing up quite near Brookfield; soldiers using the playing fields for sports and training; swift developments of Brookfield O.T.C. Most of the younger masters gone or in uniform. Every Sunday night, in the Chapel after evening service, Chatteris read out the names of old boys killed, together with short biographies. Very moving; but Chips, in the black pew under the gallery, thought: They are only names to him; he doesn't see their faces as I do. . . .

1916. . . . The Somme Battle. Twenty-three names read out one Sunday evening.

Toward the close of that catastrophic July, Chatteris talked to Chips one afternoon at Mrs. Wickett's. He was overworked and overworried and looked very ill. "To tell you the truth, Chipping, I'm not having too easy a time here. I'm thirty-nine, you know, and unmarried, and lots of people seem to think they know what I ought to do. Also, I happen to be diabetic, and couldn't pass the blindest M.O., but I don't see why I should pin a medical certificate on my front door."

Chips hadn't known anything about this; it was a shock to him, for he liked Chatteris.

The latter continued: "You see how it is. Ralston filled the place up with young men--all very good, of course--but now most of them have joined up and the substitutes are pretty dreadful, on the whole. They poured ink down a man's neck in prep one night last week--silly fool--got hysterical. I have to take classes myself, take prep for fools like that, work till midnight every night, and get cold-shouldered as a slacker on top of everything. I can't stand it much longer. If things don't improve next term I shall have a breakdown."

"I do sympathize with you," Chips said.

"I hoped you would. And that brings me to what I came here to ask you. Briefly, my suggestion is that--if you felt equal to it and would care to--how about coming back here for a while? You look pretty fit, and, of course, you know all the ropes. I don't mean a lot of hard work for you--you needn't take anything strenuously--just a few odd jobs here and there, as you choose. What I'd like you for more than anything else is not for the actual work you'd do--though that, naturally, would be very valuable--but for your help in other ways--in just *belonging* here. There's nobody ever been more popular than you were, and are still--you'd help to hold things together if there were any danger of them flying to bits. And perhaps there is that danger. . . ."

Chips answered, breathlessly and with a holy joy in his heart: "I'll come. . . ."

14

He still kept on his rooms with Mrs. Wickett; indeed, he still lived there; but every morning, about half-past ten, he put on his coat and muffler and crossed the road to the School. He felt very fit, and the actual work was not taxing. Just a few forms in Latin and Roman History--the old lessons--even the old pronunciation. The same joke about the Lex Canuleia--there was a new generation that had not heard it, and he was absurdly gratified by the success it achieved. He felt a little like a music-hall favorite returning to the boards after a positively last appearance.

They all said how marvelous it was that he knew every boy's name and face so quickly. They did not guess how closely he had kept in touch from across the road.

He was a grand success altogether. In some strange way he did, and they all knew and felt it, help things. For the first time in his life he felt *necessary*--and necessary to something that was nearest his heart. There is no sublimer feeling in the world, and it was his at last.

He made new jokes, too--about the O.T.C. and the food-rationing system and the anti-air-raid blinds that had to be fitted on all the windows. There was a mysterious kind of rissole that began to appear on the School menu on Mondays, and Chips called it *abhorrendum*-- "meat to be abhorred." The story went round--heard Chips's latest?

Chatteris fell ill during the winter of '17, and again, for the second time in his life, Chips became Acting Head of Brookfield. Then in April Chatteris died, and the Governors asked Chips if he would carry on "for the duration." He said he would, if they would refrain from appointing him officially. From that last honor, within his reach at last, he shrank instinctively, feeling himself in so many ways unequal to it. He said to Rivers: "You see, I'm not a young man and I don't want people to--um--expect a lot from me. I'm like all these new colonels and majors you see everywhere--just a war-time fluke. A ranker--that's all I am really."

1917. 1918. Chips lived through it all. He sat in the headmaster's study every morning, handling problems, dealing with plaints and requests. Out of vast experience had emerged a kindly, gentle confidence in himself. To keep a sense of proportion, that was the main thing. So much of the world was losing it; as well keep it where it had, or ought to have, a congenial home.

On Sundays in Chapel it was he who now read out the tragic list, and sometimes it was seen and heard that he was in tears over it. Well, why not, the School said; he was an old man; they might have despised anyone else for the weakness.

One day he got a letter from Switzerland, from friends there; it was heavily censored, but conveyed some news. On the following Sunday, after the names and biographies of old boys, he paused a moment and then added:--

"Those few of you who were here before the War will remember Max Staefel, the German master. He was in Germany, visiting his home, when war broke out. He was popular while he was here, and made many friends. Those who knew him will be sorry to hear that he was killed last week, on the Western Front."

He was a little pale when he sat down afterward, aware that he had done something unusual. He had consulted nobody about it, anyhow; no one else could be blamed. Later, outside the Chapel, he heard an argument:--

"On the Western Front, Chips said. Does that mean he was fighting for the Germans?"

"I suppose it does."

"Seems funny, then, to read his name out with all the others. After all, he was an *enemy.*"

"Oh, just one of Chips's ideas, I expect. The old boy still has 'em."

Chips, in his room again, was not displeased by the comment. Yes, he still had 'em--those ideas of dignity and generosity that were becoming increasingly rare in a frantic world. And he thought: Brookfield will take them, too, from me; but it wouldn't from anyone else.

Once, asked for his opinion of bayonet practice being carried on near the cricket pavilion, he answered, with that lazy, slightly asthmatic intonation that had been so often and so extravagantly imitated: "It seems--to me--umph--a very vulgar way of killing people."

41

The yarn was passed on and joyously appreciated--how Chips had told some big brass hat from the War Office that bayonet fighting was vulgar. Just like Chips. And they found an adjective for him--an adjective just beginning to be used: he was pre-War.

15

And once, on a night of full moonlight, the air-raid warning was given while Chips was taking his lower fourth in Latin. The guns began almost instantly, and, as there was plenty of shrapnel falling about outside, it seemed to Chips that they might just as well stay where they were, on the ground floor of School House. It was pretty solidly built and made as good a dugout as Brookfield could offer; and as for a direct hit, well, they could not expect to survive that, wherever they were.

So he went on with his Latin, speaking a little louder amid the reverberating crashes of the guns and the shrill whine of anti-aircraft shells. Some of the boys were nervous; few were able to be attentive. He said, gently: "It may possibly seem to you, Robertson--at this particular moment in the world's history--umph--that the affairs of Caesar in Gaul some two thousand years ago--are--umph--of somewhat secondary importance--and that--umph--the irregular conjugation of the verb *tollo* is--umph--even less important still. But believe me--umph-- my dear Robertson--that is not really the case." Just then there came a particularly loud explosion--quite near. "You cannot--umph--judge the importance of things--umph--by the noise they make. Oh dear me, no." A little chuckle. "And these things--umph--that have mattered--for thousands of years--are not going to be--snuffed out--because some stink merchant--in his laboratory--invents a new kind of mischief." Titters of nervous laughter; for Buffles, the pale, lean, and medically unfit science master, was nicknamed the Stink Merchant. Another explosion--nearer still. "Let us--um--resume our work. If it is fate that we are soon to be--umph--interrupted, let us be found employing ourselves in something--umph--really appropriate. Is there anyone who will volunteer to construe?"

Maynard, chubby, dauntless, clever, and impudent, said: "I will, sir."

"Very good. Turn to page forty and begin at the bottom line."

The explosions still continued deafeningly; the whole building shook as if it were being lifted off its foundations. Maynard found the page, which was some way ahead, and began, shrilly:--

"Genus hoc erat pugnae--this was the kind of fight--*quo se Germani exercuerant*--in which the Germans busied themselves. Oh, sir, that's good--that's really very funny indeed, sir--one of your very best--"

Laughing began, and Chips added: "Well--umph--you can see--now--that these dead languages--umph--can come to life again--sometimes--eh? Eh?"

Afterward they learned that five bombs had fallen in and around Brookfield, the nearest of them just outside the School grounds. Nine persons had been killed.

The story was told, retold, embellished. "The dear old boy never turned a hair. Even found some old tag to illustrate what was going on. Something in Caesar about the way the Germans fought. You wouldn't think there were things like that in Caesar, would you? And the way Chips laughed . . . you know the way he *does* laugh . . . the tears all running down his face . . . never seen him laugh so much. . . ."

He was a legend.

With his old and tattered gown, his walk that was just beginning to break into a stumble, his mild eyes peering over the steel-rimmed spectacles, and his quaintly humorous sayings, Brookfield would not have had an atom of him different.

November 11, 1918.

News came through in the morning; a whole holiday was decreed for the School, and the kitchen staff were implored to provide as cheerful a spread as wartime rationing permitted. There was much cheering and singing, and a bread fight across the Dining Hall. When Chips entered in the midst of the uproar there was an instant hush, and then wave upon wave of cheering; everyone gazed on him with eager, shining eyes, as on a symbol of victory. He walked to the dais, seeming as if he wished to speak; they made silence for him, but he shook his head after a moment, smiled, and walked away again.

It had been a damp, foggy day, and the walk across the quadrangle to the Dining Hall had given him a chill. The next day he was in bed with bronchitis, and stayed there till after Christmas. But already, on that night of November 11, after his visit to the Dining Hall, he had sent in his resignation to the Board of Governors.

When school reassembled after the holidays he was back at Mrs. Wickett's. At his own request there were no more farewells or presentations, nothing but a handshake with his successor and the word "acting" crossed out on official stationery. The "duration" was over.

16

And now, fifteen years after that, he could look back upon it all with a deep and sumptuous tranquillity. He was not ill, of course--only a little tired at times, and bad with his breathing during the winter months. He would not go abroad--he had once tried it, but had chanced to strike the Riviera during one of its carefully unadvertised cold spells. "I prefer--um--to get my chills--umph--in my own country," he used to say, after that. He had to take care of himself when there were east winds, but autumn and winter were not really so bad; there were warm fires, and books, and you could look forward to the summer. It was the summer that he liked best, of course; apart from the weather, which suited him, there were the continual visits of old boys. Every weekend some of them motored up to Brookfield and called at his house. Sometimes they tired him, if too many came at once; but he did not really mind; he could always rest and sleep afterward. And he enjoyed their visits--more than anything else in the world that was still to be enjoyed. "Well, Gregson--umph--I remember you--umph--always late for everything--eh--eh? Perhaps you'll be late in growing old--umph--like me--umph--eh?" And later, when he was alone again and Mrs. Wickett came in to clear away the tea things: "Mrs. Wickett, young Gregson called--umph--you remember him, do you? Tall boy with spectacles. Always late. Umph. Got a job with the--umph--League of Nations--where--I suppose--his--um--dilatoriness--won't be noticeable--eh?"

And sometimes, when the bell rang for call-over, he would go to the window and look across the road and over the School fence and see, in the distance, the thin line of boys filing past the bench. New times, new names . . . but the old ones still remained . . . Jefferson, Jennings, Jolyon, Jupp, Kingsley Primus, Kingsley Secundus, Kingsley Tertius, Kingston . . . where are you all, where have you all gone to? . . . Mrs. Wickett, bring me a cup of tea just before prep, will you, please?

The post-War decade swept through with a clatter of change and maladjustments; Chips, as he lived through it, was profoundly disappointed when he looked abroad. The Ruhr, Chanak, Corfu; there was enough to be uneasy about in the world. But near him, at Brookfield, and even, in a wider sense, in England, there was something that charmed his heart because it was old--and had survived. More and more he saw the rest of the world as a vast disarrangement for which England had sacrificed enough--and perhaps too much. But he was satisfied with Brookfield. It was rooted in things that had stood the test of time and change and war. Curious, in this deeper sense, how little it *had* changed. Boys were a politer race; bullying was non-existent; there was more swearing and cheating. There was a more genuine friendliness between master and boy--less pomposity on the one side, less unctuousness on the other. One of the new masters, fresh from Oxford, even let the Sixth call him by his Christian name. Chips didn't hold with that; indeed, he was just a little bit shocked. "He might as well--umph--sign his terminal reports--umph--'yours affectionately'-- eh--eh?" he told somebody.

During the General Strike of 1926, Brookfield boys loaded motor vans with foodstuffs. When it was all over, Chips felt stirred emotionally as he had not been since the War. Something had happened, something whose ultimate significance had yet to be reckoned. But one thing was clear: England had burned her fire in her own grate again. And when, at a Speech Day function that year, an American visitor laid stress on the vast sums that the strike had cost the country, Chips answered: "Yes, but--umph--advertisement--always *is* costly."

"Advertisement?"

"Well, wasn't it--umph--advertisement--and very fine advertisement--too? A whole week of it--umph--and not a life lost--not a shot fired! Your country would have--umph--spilt more blood in--umph-- raiding a single liquor saloon!"

Laughter . . . laughter . . . wherever he went and whatever he said, there was laughter. He had earned the reputation of being a great jester, and jests were expected of him. Whenever he rose to speak at a meeting, or even when he talked across a table, people prepared their minds and faces for the joke. They listened in a mood to be amused and it was easy to satisfy them. They laughed sometimes before he came to the point. "Old Chips was in fine form," they would say, afterward. "Marvelous the way he can always see the funny side of things. . . ."

After 1929, Chips did not leave Brookfield--even for Old Boys' dinners in London. He was afraid of chills, and late nights began to tire him too much. He came across to the School, however, on fine days; and he still kept up a wide and continual hospitality in his room. His faculties were all unimpaired, and he had no personal worries of any kind. His income was more than he needed to spend, and his small capital, invested in gilt-edged stocks, did not suffer when the slump set in. He gave a lot of money away--to people who called on him with a hard-luck story, to various School funds, and also to the Brookfield mission. In 1930 he made his will. Except for legacies to the mission and to Mrs. Wickett, he left all he had to found an open scholarship to the School.

1931. . . . 1932. . . .

"What do you think of Hoover, sir?"

"Do you think we shall ever go back to gold?"

"How d'you feel about things in general, sir? See any break in the clouds?"

"When's the tide going to turn, Chips, old boy? You ought to know, with all your experience of things."

They all asked him questions, as if he were some kind of prophet and encyclopedia combined--more even than that, for they liked their answer dished up as a joke. He would say:--

"Well, Henderson, when I was--umph--a much younger man--there used to be someone who--um--promised people ninepence for four-pence. I don't know that anybody--umph--ever got it, but--umph--our present rulers seem--um--to have solved the problem how to give--umph--fourpence for ninepence."

Laughter.

Sometimes, when he was strolling about the School, small boys of the cheekier kind would ask him questions, merely for the fun of getting Chips's "latest" to retail.

"Please, sir, what about the Five-Year Plan?"

"Sir, do you think Germany wants to fight another war?"

"Have you been to the new cinema, sir? I went with my people the other day. Quite a grand affair for a small place like Brookfield. They've got a Wurlitzer."

"And what--umph--on earth--is a Wurlitzer?"

"It's an organ, sir--a cinema organ."

"Dear me. . . . I've seen the name on the hoardings, but I always--umph--imagined--it must be some kind of--umph--sausage."

Laughter. . . . Oh, there's a new Chips joke, you fellows, a perfectly lovely one. I was gassing to the old boy about the new cinema, and . . .

17

He sat in his front parlor at Mrs. Wickett's on a November afternoon in thirty-three. It was cold and foggy, and he dare not go out. He had not felt too well since Armistice Day; he fancied he might have caught a slight chill during the Chapel service. Merivale had been that morning for his usual fortnightly chat. "Everything all right? Feeling hearty? That's the style--keep indoors this weather--there's a lot of flu about. Wish I could have your life for a day or two."

His life . . . and what a life it had been! The whole pageant of it swung before him as he sat by the fire that afternoon. The things he had done and seen: Cambridge in the sixties; Great Gable on an August morning; Brookfield at all times and seasons throughout the years. And, for that matter, the things he had *not* done, and would never do now that he had left them too late--he had never traveled by air, for instance, and he had never been to a talkie-show. So that he was both more and less experienced than the youngest new boy at the School might well be; and that, that paradox of age and youth, was what the world called progress.

Mrs. Wickett had gone out, visiting relatives in a neighbourly village; she had left the tea things ready on the table, with bread and butter and extra cups laid out in case anybody called. On such a day, however, visitors were not very likely; with the fog thickening hourly outside, he would probably be alone.

But no. About a quarter to four a ring came, and Chips, answering the front door himself (which he oughtn't to have done), encountered a rather small boy wearing a Brookfield cap and an expression of anxious timidity. "Please, sir," he began, "does Mr. Chips live here?"

"Umph--you'd better come inside," Chips answered. And in his room a moment later he added: "I am--umph--the person you want. Now what can I--umph--do for you?"

"I was told you wanted me, sir."

Chips smiled. An old joke--an old leg-pull, and he, of all people, having made so many old jokes in his time, ought not to complain. And it amused him to cap their joke, as it were, with one of his own; to let them see that he could keep his end up, even yet. So he said, with eyes twinkling: "Quite right, my boy. I wanted you to take tea with me. Will you--umph--sit down by the fire? Umph--I don't think I have seen your face before. How is that?"

"I've only just come out of the sanatorium, sir--I've been there since the beginning of term with measles."

"Ah, that accounts for it."

Chips began his usual ritualistic blending of tea from the different caddies; luckily there was half a walnut cake with pink icing in the cupboard. He found out that the boy's name was Linford, that he lived in Shropshire, and that he was the first of his family at Brookfield.

"You know--umph--Linford--you'll like Brookfield--when you get used to it. It's not half such an awful place--as you imagine. You're a bit afraid of it--um, yes--eh? So was I, my dear boy--at first. But that was--um--a long time ago. Sixty-three years ago--umph--to be precise. When I--um--first went into Big Hall and--um--I saw all those boys--I tell you--I was quite scared. Indeed--umph--I don't think I've ever been so scared in my life. Not even when--umph--the Germans bombed us-- during the War. But--umph--it didn't last long--the scared feeling, I mean. I soon made myself--um--at home."

"Were there a lot of other new boys that term, sir?" asked Linford shyly.

"Eh? But--God bless my soul--I wasn't a boy at all--I was a man--a young man of twenty-two! And the next time you see a young man--a new master--taking his first prep in Big Hall--umph--just think--what it feels like!"

"But if you were twenty-two then, sir--"

"Yes? Eh?"

"You must be--very old--now, sir."

Chips laughed quietly and steadily to himself. It was a good joke.

"Well--umph--I'm certainly--umph--no chicken."

He laughed quietly to himself for a long time.

Then he talked of other matters, of Shropshire, of schools and school life in general, of the news in that day's papers. "You're grow-ing up into--umph--a very cross sort of world, Linford. Maybe it will have got over some of its--umph--crossness--by the time you're ready for it. Let's hope so--umph--at any rate. . . . Well . . ." And with a glance at the clock he delivered himself of his old familiar formula. "I'm--umph--sorry--you can't stay . . ."

At the front door he shook hands.

"Good-bye, my boy."

And the answer came, in a shrill treble: "Good-bye, Mr. Chips. . . ."

Chips sat by the fire again, with those words echoing along the corridors of his mind. "Good-bye, Mr. Chips. . . ." An old leg-pull, to make new boys think that his name was really Chips; the joke was almost traditional. He did not mind. "Good-bye, Mr. Chips. . . ." He remembered that on the eve of his wedding day Kathie had used that same phrase, mocking him gently for the seriousness he had had in those days. He thought: Nobody would call me serious today, that's very certain. . . .

Suddenly the tears began to roll down his cheeks--an old man's failing; silly, perhaps, but he couldn't help it. He felt very tired; talking to Linford like that had quite exhausted him. But he was glad he had met Linford. Nice boy. Would do well.

Over the fog-laden air came the bell for call-over, tremulous and muffled. Chips looked at the window, graying into twilight; it was time to light up. But as soon as he began to move he felt that he couldn't; he was too tired; and, anyhow, it didn't matter. He leaned back in his chair. No chicken--eh, well--that was true enough. And it had been amusing about Linford. A neat score off the jokers who had sent the boy over. Good-bye, Mr. Chips . . . odd, though, that he should have said it just like that. . . .

18

When he awoke, for he seemed to have been asleep, he found himself in bed; and Merivale was there, stooping over him and smiling. "Well, you old ruffian--feeling all right? That was a fine shock you gave us!"

Chips murmured, after a pause, and in a voice that surprised him by its weakness: "Why--um--what--what has happened?"

"Merely that you threw a faint. Mrs. Wickett came in and found you--lucky she did. You're all right now. Take it easy. Sleep again if you feel inclined."

He was glad someone had suggested such a good idea. He felt so weak that he wasn't even puzzled by the details of the business--how they had got him upstairs, what Mrs. Wickett had said, and so on. But then, suddenly, at the other side of the bed, he saw Mrs. Wickett. She was smiling. He thought: God bless my soul, what's she doing up here? And then, in the shadows behind Merivale, he saw Cartwright, the new Head (he thought of him as "new," even though he had been at Brookfield since 1919), and old Buffles, commonly called "Roddy." Funny, the way they were all here. He felt: Anyhow, I can't be bothered to wonder why about anything. I'm going to go to sleep.

But it wasn't sleep, and it wasn't quite wakefulness, either; it was a sort of in-between state, full of dreams and faces and voices. Old scenes and old scraps of tunes: a Mozart trio that Kathie had once played in--cheers and laughter and the sound of guns--and, over it all, Brookfield bells, Brookfield bells. "So you see, if Miss Plebs wanted Mr. Patrician to marry her . . . yes, you can, you liar. . . ." Joke . . . Meat to be abhorred. . . . Joke . . . That you, Max? Yes, come in. What's the news from the Fatherland? . . . *O mihi praeteritos* . . . Ralston said I was slack and inefficient--but they couldn't manage without me. . . . *Obile heres ago fortibus es in aro* . . . Can you translate that, any of you? . . . It's a joke. . . .

Once he heard them talking about him in the room.

Cartwright was whispering to Merivale. "Poor old chap--must have lived a lonely sort of life, all by himself."

Merivale answered: "Not always by himself. He married, you know."

"Oh, did he? I never knew about that."

"She died. It must have been--oh, quite thirty years ago. More, possibly."

"Pity. Pity he never had any children."

And at that, Chips opened his eyes as wide as he could and sought to attract their attention. It was hard for him to speak out loud, but he managed to murmur something, and they all looked round and came nearer to him.

He struggled, slowly, with his words. "What--was that--um--you were saying--about me--just now?"

Old Buffles smiled and said: "Nothing at all, old chap--nothing at all--we were just wondering when you were going to wake out of your beauty sleep."

"But--umph--I heard you--you were talking about me--"

"Absolutely nothing of any consequence, my dear fellow--really, I give you my word. . . ."

"I thought I heard you--one of you--saying it was a pity--umph--a pity I never had--any children . . . eh? . . . But I have, you know . . . I have . . ."

The others smiled without answering, and after a pause Chips began a faint and palpitating chuckle.

"Yes--umph--I have," he added, with quavering merriment. "Thousands of 'em . . . thousands of 'em . . . and all boys."

And then the chorus sang in his ears in final harmony, more grandly and sweetly than he had ever heard it before, and more comfortingly too. . . . Pettifer, Pollett, Porson, Potts, Pullman, Purvis, Pym-Wilson, Radlett, Rapson, Reade, Reaper, Reddy Primus . . . come round me now, all of you, for a last word and a joke. . . . Harper, Haslett, Hatfield, Hatherley . . . my last joke . . . did you hear it? Did it make you laugh? . . . Bone, Boston, Bovey, Bradford, Bradley, Bramhall-Anderson . . . wherever you are, whatever has happened, give me this moment with you . . . this last moment . . . my boys . . .

And soon Chips was asleep.

James Hilton

He seemed so peaceful that they did not disturb him to say good-night; but in the morning, as the School bell sounded for breakfast, Brookfield had the news. "Brookfield will never forget his lovableness," said Cartwright, in a speech to the School. Which was absurd, because all things are forgotten in the end. But Linford, at any rate, will remember and tell the tale: "I said good-bye to Chips the night before he died. . . ."

THE END

To You, Mr. Chips

James Hilton

CHAPTER ONE

A CHAPTER OF AUTOBIOGRAPHY

If I use the word 'I' a good deal in these pages, it is not from self-importance, but because I would rather talk about my own schooldays than generalise about school. Schooling is perhaps the most universal of all experiences, but it is also one of the most individual. (Here I am, generalising already!) No two schools are alike, but more than that--a school with two hundred pupils is really two hundred schools, and among them, almost certainly, are somebody's long-remembered heaven and somebody else's hell. So that I must not conceal, but rather lay stress on the first personal pronouns. The schools I write of were *my* schools; to others at the same schools at the same time, everything may have been different.

I went to three schools altogether--an elementary school, a grammar school, and a public school. I matriculated at London University and spent four years at Christ's College, Cambridge. Thus, from the age of six, when my mother led me through suburban streets for presentation to the headmistress of the nearest Infants' Department, up to the age of twenty-three, when I left Cambridge supposedly equipped for the world and its problems, the process called my education was going on. Seventeen years--quite a large slice out of a life, when you come to think about it. And yet the ways I have earned my living since--by writing newspaper articles, novels, and film scenarios--were not taught me at any of these schools and colleges. Furthermore, though I won scholarships and passed examinations, I do not think I now remember more than twenty per cent of all I learned during these seventeen years, and I do not think I could now scrape through any of the examinations I passed after the age of twelve.

Nor was there any sort of co-ordination between my three schools and the university. For this, nobody was to blame in a free country. To some extent, I learned what I liked; to a greater extent, my teachers taught me what they liked. In my time I 'took,' as they say, practically every subject takable. At the elementary school, for instance, I spent an hour a week on 'botany,' which was an excuse for wandering through Epping Forest in charge of a master who, in his turn, regarded the hour as an excuse for a pleasant smoke in the open air. The result is that Botany to me today stands for just a few words like 'calyx,' 'stamen,' and 'capillary attraction,' plus the memory of lovely hours amidst trees and bracken. I do not complain.

Again, at the grammar school I spent six hours a week for three years at an occupation called 'Chemistry,' and all these hours have left me with nothing but a certain skill in blowing glass tubes into various shapes. In mathematics I went as far as the calculus, but I do not think I could be quite sure nowadays of solving a hard quadratic equation. Of languages I learned (enough to pass examinations in them) Latin, Greek, French, and German. I suppose I could still read Virgil or Sophocles with the help of a dictionary, but I do not do so, because it would give me no pleasure. My French and German are of the kind that is understood by sympathetic Frenchmen and Germans who know English.

The only school-learning of which I remember a good deal belongs to English Literature, History, and Music; but even in these fields my knowledge is roving rather than academic, and I could no longer discuss with any degree of accuracy the debt of Shakespeare to Saxo-Grammaticus or the statute *De Heretico Comburendo.* In fact, although I am, in the titular sense, a Scholar of my college, I do not feel myself to be very scholarly. But give me a new theory about Emily Brontë or read me a pamphlet about war and peace, and I will tell you whether, in my view, the author is worth listening to. To make up for all I have forgotten, there is this that I have acquired, and I call it sophistication since it is not quite the same thing as learning. It is the flexible armour of doubt in an age when too many people are certain.

What all this amounts to, whether my seventeen years were well spent, whether I am a good or a bad example of what schooling can do, whether I should have been a better citizen if I had gone to work at fourteen, I cannot say. I can only reply in the manner of the youth who, on being asked if he had been educated at Eton, replied: 'That is a matter of opinion.'

A CHAPTER OF AUTOBIOGRAPHY

The elementary school was in one of the huge dormitory suburbs of north-east London--a suburb which people from Hampstead or Chelsea would think entirely characterless, but which, if one lived in it for twenty years as I did, revealed a delicate and by no means unlikeable quality of its own. I am still a young man, and I suppose that for the next twenty years people will go on calling me 'one of our younger novelists'; but whenever nowadays I pass by that elementary school, I realise what an age it is since I breathed its prevalent smell of ink, strong soap, and wet clothes. Just over a quarter of a century, to be precise, but it cannot be measured by that reckoning. The world today looks back on the pre-War world as a traveller may look back through a railway tunnel to the receding pinpoint of light in the distance. It is more than the past; it is already a legend.

To this legend my earliest recollections of school life belong. My father was the headmaster of another school in the same town, and I was a good deal petted and favoured by his colleagues. There were quite a few dirty and ragged boys in the class of seventy or so; the school itself was badly heated and badly lit; schoolbooks were worn and smeary because every boy had to follow the words with his finger as he read--an excusable rule, for it was the only way the teacher could see at a glance if his multitude were all paying attention. He was certainly not to blame because I found his reading lessons a bore. At the time that I was spelling out 'cat-sat-on-the-mat' stuff at school, I was racing through Dickens, Thackeray, and Jules Verne at home.

The school curriculum had its oddities. Mathematics was divided into Arithmetic, Algebra, and Mensuration. (Why this last had a special name and subdivision, I have no idea.) Geography consisted largely of learning the special names of capes, bays, countries, and county towns. When a teacher once told me that Cardigan Bay was the largest in Great Britain, I remember asking him promptly what was the smallest. He was somewhat baffled. But I have always been interested in miniature things, and perhaps I was right in supposing that England's smallest bay, were it to be identified would be worth knowing. This teacher gave me full marks, however, because I attained great proficiency in copying maps with a fine-nibbed pen--a practice which enabled me to outline all the coasts with what appeared to be a fringe of stubbly hairs.

I was not so good at history because, in the beginning I could not make head or tail of most of it. When I read that So-and-so 'gathered his army and laid waste to the country,' I could not imagine what it meant. I had heard of gathering flowers and laying an egg, but these other kinds of gathering and laying were more mystifying, and nobody bothered to explain them to me. They remained just phrases that one had to learn and repeat. I was also puzzled by the vast number of people in history who were put to death because they would not change their religion; indeed, the entire fuss about religion throughout history was inexplicable to a boy whose father played the organ at a Congregational Church during the reign of Edward the Seventh.

Since then I have helped to write school history books and have found out for myself the immense difficulty of teaching the subject to children. It is not the words only that have to be simplified, but the ideas--and if you over-simplify ideas, you often falsify them. Hence the almost inevitable perversion of history into a series of gags, anecdotes, labels--that So-and-so was a 'good' king, that Henry the Eighth had six wives and Cromwell a wart on his nose, that the messenger came to Wolfe crying 'They run, they run' and that Nelson clapped the glass to his sightless eye. When later I studied history seriously for a university scholarship, I was continually amazed by the discovery that historical personages behaved, for the most part, with reasonable motivation for their actions and not like the Marx Brothers in a costume-play.

'Scripture' was another subject I did not excel at. It consisted of a perfunctory reading of a daily passage from the Bible; and our Bibles were always dirty, ragged, and bound in black. They left me with an impression of a book I did not want to handle, much less to read; it is only during the past ten years that I have read the Bible for pleasure. Our school Bibles also suffered from too small print; some of the words in the text were in italics and nobody explained to me that the reason for this concerned scholars more than schoolboys. Not long ago I heard a local preacher who seemed to me, when reading from the Psalms, to give certain sentences an unusual rhythm, and on inquiry I found that he had always imagined that the words in italics had to be accented! Why not print an abridged and large-print Bible for schools, consolidating groups of verses into paragraphs, and finally binding the whole as attractively as any other book? Maybe this has been done, and I am out of date for suggesting it.

Another oddity of my early schooldays was something called a free-arm system of hand writing--it consisted of holding the wrist rigid and moving the pen by means of the forearm muscle. I can realise now that somebody got his living by urging this fad on schoolmasters who liked to be thought modern or were amenable to sales-talk; I thought it nonsense at the time and employed some resolution in not learning it.

Perhaps the chief thing I *did* learn at my first school was that my father (then earning about six pounds a week) was a rich man. When, later on, I went to schools at which he seemed (in the same comparative sense) a poor man, I had the whole social system already sketch-mapped in my mind, and I did not think it perfect.

The school was perhaps a better-than-average example, both structurally and educationally, of its type; so I can only conjecture what conditions were like at the worst schools in the worst parts of London. I do know that there have been tremendous improvements since those days; that free meals and medical inspections have smoothed down the rougher differences between the poor man's child and others; that, under Hitler and Stalin and Neville Chamberlain alike, the starved and ragged urchin has become a rarity. Such a trend is common throughout the world and we need not be complacent about it, since its motive is as much militaristic as humanitarian. But it does remain, intrinsically, a mighty good thing. I believe I would have benefited a lot from the improved elementary school of today. I might not have learned any more, but I should probably have had better teeth.

From the elementary school I went to a grammar school in the same suburb. It was an old foundation (as old as Harrow), but it had come down in the world. I had the luck to have for a form-master a man who was very deaf. I call it 'luck,' because he was an excellent teacher and would probably have attached himself to a much better school but for his affliction. As it was, his discipline was the best in the school--with the proviso, of course, that his eyes had to do vigilance for his ears. The result was that, in addition to Latin, English, and History, I gained in his class another proficiency that has never been of the slightest use to me since--ventriloquism.

I was devoted to that man (and I am sure he never guessed it). His frown could spoil my day, his rare slanting smile could light it up. I was conceited enough to think that he took some special interest in me, just because he read out my essays publicly to the class; and after I sent him in an essay I used to picture the excitement he must feel on reading it. It did not occur to me that, like most good professionals (as opposed to amateurs), he did his job conscientiously but without hysterical enthusiasm, and that during out-of-school hours he would rather have a drink and a chat with a friend than read the best schoolboy's essay ever written.

Once he wrote on the blackboard some sentences for parsing and analysis. Among them was: 'Dreams such as thine pass now like evening clouds before me; when I think how beautiful they seem, 'tis but to feel how soon they fade, how fast the night shuts in.' I was so struck with this that I sat for a long time thinking of it; and presently, noticing my idleness, he asked me rather sharply why I wasn't working. I couldn't tell him, partly because I hardly knew, partly because any answer would have had to be shouted at the top of my voice on account of his deafness. I let him think I was just lazy, yet in my heart I never forgave him for not understanding.

Children are merciless--as much in what they expect as in what they offer. Not only will they bait unmercifully a schoolmaster who lacks the power to discipline them, but they lavish the most fantastic and unreasonable adorations. The utmost bond of lover and mistress is less than the comprehension a boy expects from a schoolmaster whom he has singled out for worship. I cannot imagine any more desperate situation for a school than the one in which this grammar school found itself. (It has since moved to another site, so nothing I say can bear any current reflection.) Flanked on one side by a pickle-factory, it shared its other aspects between the laundry of the municipal baths and a busy thoroughfare lined by market-stalls. Personally I rather liked the rococo liveliness of such surroundings. I grew used to the pervading smell of chutney and steaming bath-towels, to the cries of costers selling oranges and cough-drops, and it was fun to step out of the classroom on winter evenings and search a book-barrow lit by naphtha-flares, or listen to a Hindu peddling a corn-cure. And there was a roaring music-hall nearby, with jugglers and Little Tich and Gertie Gitana; and on Friday nights outside the municipal baths a strange-eyed long haired soap-boxer talked anarchism. Somehow it was all rather like Nijni Novgorod, though I have never seen Nijni Novgorod.

I probably learned more in the street than I did in the school, but the latter did leave me with a good grammatical foundation in Latin, as well as a certain facility in the use of woodworking tools. (Since then I have usually made my own bookshelves.) One of the teachers made us learn three solid pages of Sir Walter Scott's prose from *The Talisman* (a passage, I still remember, beginning--'Beside his couch stood Thomas de Vaux, in face, attitude and manner the strongest possible contrast to the suffering monarch'); the intention, I suppose, was that we might somehow learn to write a bit more like Scott; but as I did not want to write like Scott at all, the effort of memory was rather wasted.

I worked hard at this grammar school, chiefly because homework was piled on by various masters acting independently of each other. I was a quick worker, but often I did not finish till nearly midnight, and how the slower workers managed I can only imagine. I have certainly never worked so hard in my life since, and it has often struck me as remarkable that an age that restricts the hours of child-employment in industry should permit the much harder routine of schoolwork by day and homework in the evenings. A twelve-hour shift is no less harmful for a boy or girl because it is spent over books; indeed, the overworked errand-boy is less to be pitied. Unless conditions have changed (and I know that in some schools they haven't), there are still many thousands of child-slaves in this country.

The chief reason for such slavery is probably the life-and-death struggle for examination distinctions in which most schools are compelled to take part. And that again is based on the whole idea of pedagogy which has survived, with less change than one might think, from the Middle Ages. It is perhaps a pity that the average school curriculum fits a pupil for one profession better than any other--that of school-mastering. It is a pity because the clever schoolboy is tempted into the only profession in which his store of knowledge is of immediate practical value in getting him a job, and is then tempted to emphasise the value of passing on precisely that same knowledge to others. He is somewhat in the position of a shopkeeper whose aim is less to sell people what they need than to get rid of what he has in stock. The circle is vexatious, but I would not call it vicious, because I do not think that the whole or even the chief value of a schoolmaster can be measured by the knowledge he imparts. Much of that knowledge will be forgotten, anyway, and far more easily than the influence of a cultured and liberal-minded personality. Indeed, in a world in which the practical people are so busy doing things that had better not be done at all, there may even be some advantage in the sheer mundane uselessness of a classical education. Better the vagaries of 'tollo' than those of a new poison gas; better to learn and forget our Latin verbs than to learn and remember our experimental chemistry; better by far we should forget and smile than that we should remember and be sad.

So I defend (somewhat tepidly) a classical education for the very reason that so many people attack it. It is of small practical value in a world whose practical values are mostly wrong; it is 'waste time' in a world whose time had better be wasted than spent in most of its present activities. My Mr. Chips, who went on with his Latin lesson while the Zeppelins were dropping bombs, was aware that he was 'wasting' the possibly last moments of himself and his pupils, but he believed that at any rate he was wasting them with dignity and without malice.

The War broke out while I was still at the suburban grammar school; during that last lovely June of the pre-War era, I had won a scholarship to a public school in Hertfordshire. I remember visiting a charming little country town and being quartered there at a temperance hotel in company with other entrants. The school sent its German master to look after us--a pleasant, sandy-haired, kind-faced man with iron-rimmed spectacles and a guttural accent--almost the caricatured Teuton whom, two months later, we were all trying to hate. I forget his name, and as I never saw him or the school again, I do not know what happened to him.

I never saw the place again because my father, poring over the prospectus, discovered that the school possessed both a rifle-range and an Officers' Training Corps--symbols of the War that, above all things, he hated. He had been a pacifist long before he ever called himself one (indeed, he never liked the term), and it is literally true to say that he would not hurt a fly--for my mother could never use a fly-swat if he were in the same room. Yet I know that if anyone had broken into our house and attacked my mother or me--the kind of problem put two years later by truculent army officers to nervous conscientious objectors--it would have been no problem at all to my father; he would have died in battle. He was no sentimentalist. When a bad disciplinarian on his teaching staff once asked him what he (my father) would say if a boy squirted ink at him, my father answered promptly: 'It isn't what I'd *say,* it's what I'd *do.*' And he would have--though I cannot imagine that he ever had to. Boys in his presence always gave an impression of enjoying liberty without taking liberties. He was a strong man, physically--a good swimmer, a good cricketer, nothing of the weakling about him; and to call him a pacifist is merely to exemplify his fighting capacity for lost causes. It never occurred to me then, and it rarely occurs to me now, that any of his ideas were fundamentally wrong. He was and happily is still a mixture of Cobbett and Tagore with a dash of aboriginal John Bull.

I was just fourteen then--the age at which most boys in England leave school and go to work. It was the first autumn of the War, when our enthusiasm for the Russian steamroller led us to deplore the fact that we could not read Dostoievski in the original; so with this idea in mind, I began to learn Russian and tried for a job in a Russian bank in London. Worse still, I nearly got it. If I had, it is excitingly possible that I should have been sent to Russia and been there during the Revolution; but far more probable that I should have added figures in a City office until the bank eventually went out of business.

My father, however, was beginning to dally again with the idea of a public school for me, and soon conceived the idea that since he could not make up his mind, I should choose a school for myself. So I toured England on this eccentric but interesting quest and learned how to work out train journeys from York to Cheltenham and from Brighton to Sherborne, how to pick good but cheap hotels in small towns, and how to convince a headmaster that if I didn't get a good impression of his school, I should unhesitatingly cross it off my list. When I look back upon these visits, I am inclined to praise my father for a stroke of originality of which both he and I were altogether unaware. It would, perhaps, be a good thing if boys were given more say in choosing their own schools. It certainly would be a good thing if headmasters cared more about the impressions they made on boys and less about the impressions they made on parents. Only a few of the headmasters to whom I explained my mission were elaborately sarcastic and refused to see me.

Eventually I spent a week-end at Cambridge and liked the town and university atmosphere so much that I finally made the choice, despite the fact that the school there possessed both the rifle-range and the cadet corps. Relying on the fact that my father was both forgetful and unobservant, I said nothing about this at home, got myself entered for the school, and joined it half-way through the summer term of 1915.

You will here remark that your sympathies are entirely with the headmasters who were sarcastic, and that I must have been an exceptionally priggish youngster. I shall not disagree, except to remark that, prig or not, I am grateful to those pedagogues who showed me over their establishment with as much bored and baffled courtesy as they might have accorded to a foreign general or the wife of a speech-day celebrity.

Not so long ago I read a symposium contributed by various young and youngish writers about their own personal experiences at public schools. These experiences ranged from the mildly tolerable to the downright disgusting; indeed, the whole effect of the book was to create pity for any sensitive, intelligent youngster consigned to such environment. I do not for a moment dispute the sincerity of this symposium. I am prepared to believe almost any specific detail about almost any specific school. Of my own school I could say, for instance, that some of its hygienic conditions would have aroused the indignation of every Socialist M.P. if only they had been found in a Durham or a South Wales mining village. I could specify, quite truthfully, that the main latrines were next to the dining-room; that we were apt to find a drowned rat in the bath-tub if we left the water to stand overnight; that in winter the moisture ran down walls that had obviously been built without a dampcourse; that the school sanatorium was an incredible Victorian villa at the other end of the town, hopelessly unsuited to its purpose. These things have been remedied since, but they were true enough in my time--and what of it? Their enumeration cannot present a true impression of my school or of any school, because a school is something more than the buildings of which it is composed.

I know that a visiting American would have been sheerly horrified by the plumbing and drainage, but no more horrified than I am when, having duly admired some magnificent million-dollar scholastic outfit on the plains of the Middle West, I learn that it offers a degree in instalment-selling and pays its athletic coach twice as much as its headmaster. This seems to me the worst kind of modern lunacy. Better to have rats in the bathtub than bats in the belfry.

I am, as I said just now, prepared to believe almost any specific detail about almost any specific school. But a book or even a page of specific details must be considered with due allowance for the age and character of the writer. Many men after middle-life remember nothing but good about their schools. Their prevalent mood by that time has become so nostalgic for past youth that anything connected with it acquires a halo, so that even a beating bitterly resented at the time becomes, in retrospect, a rather jolly business. (Most of the 'jolly' words for corporal punishment--'spank', 'whack,' etc., were, I suspect, invented by sentimentalists of over forty.) The kind of man who feels like this is often the kind that makes a material success of life and whose autobiography, written or ghost-written, exudes the main idea that 'school made him what he was'--than which, of course, he can conceive no higher praise.

On the other hand, in reading the school reminiscences of youths who have just left it, one should remember that the typical schoolboy is inarticulate, and that by putting any such reminiscences on paper the writer is proving himself, *ipso facto,* to be untypical. In other words, recollections of schools are apt to be written either by elderly successful men who remember nothing but good, or by youths who, by their very skill in securing an audience at such an early age, argue themselves to have been unlike the average schoolboy.

There is nothing for it, therefore, but to be frankly personal and leave others to make whatever allowances they may think necessary.

I am thirty-seven years of age. I do not think I am old enough yet to feel that school was a good place because I was young in it, or self-satisfied enough to feel that school was a good place because it 'made me what I am.' (In any case, I do not think it did make me what I am, whatever that may be.) But I enjoyed my schooldays, on the whole, and if I had a son I dare say I would send him to my old school, if only because I would not know what else to do with him.

I was not a typical schoolboy, and the fact that I was happy at (shall we say?) Brookfield argues that the school tolerated me even more generously that I tolerated it. Talking to other men about their schooldays, I have often thought that Brookfield must have been less rigid than many schools in enforcing conformity to type. Perhaps the fact that it was, in the religious sense, a Nonconformist school helped to distil a draught of personal freedom, that even wartime could not dissipate. At any rate, I did not join the almost compulsory Officers' Training Corps, despite the fact that the years were 1914-1918. My reasons for keeping out (which I did not conceal) were simply that I disliked military training and had no aptitude for it. Lest anyone should picture my stand as a heroic one, I should add that it was really no stand at all; nobody persecuted me--if they had, no doubt I should have joined.

When later I was called up for military service I responded, chiefly because my friends were in the army and I guessed I should be happier with them there than on committees of anti-war societies with people whose views I mainly held. If this seems an illogical reason, I shall agree, with the proviso that it is also a more civilised reason than a desire to kill Germans.

I did not conceal my views about the War, but I did conceal my general feeling about games. I was, in this respect, a complete hypocrite. I have never been able to take the slightest interest in most games, partly because I am no good at them myself; I like outdoor pursuits such as walking, sea-bathing, and mountaineering, but the competitive excitements of cup-finals and test matches bore me to exasperation. The only contest even remotely athletic into which I ever entered with zest was the saying of the Latin grace at my Cambridge college; it was a long grace, and I was told (how accurately I cannot say) that I lowered the all-time speed record from sixteen to fourteen and a fifth seconds. At Brookfield, however, grace was said by the masters, so that my prowess in this field remained unsuspected, even by myself. The craze for clipping fifths of seconds raged elsewhere. Most of my friends were tremendously concerned about 'the hundred yards' and the various School and House matches, and I would not for the world have let them know that I cared nothing about such things at all. Sometimes, if there was absolutely no one else left to fill the team, I took part in some very junior housematch, and I always hoped that my side would lose, because then I should not have to play in any sub-sequent game. Outwardly, however, I pretended to share all the normal enthusiasms over victory and despairs over defeat; and I think I carried it off pretty well. There is always some ultimate thing you must do when you are in Rome, even if the Romans are exceptionally broad-minded.

I never received corporal punishment at Brookfield; I was never bullied; I never had a fight with anybody; and the only trouble I got into was for breaking bounds. I used to enjoy lazy afternoons at the Orchard, Grantchester, with strawberries and cream for tea; I liked to attend Evensong at King's College Chapel; I liked to smoke cigarettes in cafés. Most of these diversions were against school rules, and I have an idea that often when I was seen breaking them, the observer tactful-ly closed an eye. Perhaps it was realised that my desire for personal freedom did not incline me to foment general rebellion. Many things that I care about do not attract others at all, and awareness of this has always made me reluctant to exalt my own particular cravings into the dimensions of a crusade. On the whole, I thought the school discipline reasonable, if occasionally irksome, and when I transgressed I did so without either resentment or regret.

Strangely, perhaps, since I was not 'the type,' I was quite happy at Brookfield. The very things I disliked (games, for instance) brightened some days by darkening others; I have rarely been so happy in my life as when, taking a hot bath after a football game in which I hardly touched the ball, I reflected that no one would compel me to indulge in such preposterous pseudo-activity for another forty-eight hours. I had many acquaintances, and a few close friends with whom my relation-ship was as unselfish as any I have experienced since in my life. I do not think I had any particular enemies, and I got on well enough with authority. Despite the sexual aberrations that are supposed to thrive at boarding-schools, I never succumbed to any, nor was I ever tempted. I played the piano dashingly rather than accurately at speech-day con-certs, breakfasted with the Head once a term, argued for or against capital punishment (I forget which) in the school debating society, and cycled many windy miles along the fenland lanes.

The magic of youth is in the sudden unfolding of vistas, the lifting of mists from the mile-high territory of manhood. It sometimes falls to me nowadays to read a fine new book by a new writer, but never to discover a whole shelf of new books at once--as happened after I had first read *Clayhanger*. New worlds are for the young to explore; later one is glad of a new room or even of a view from a new window. That the worlds were not seen in proper focus, while the room or the view may be, does not entirely compensate for the slowing of excitement-- for the loss of a mood in which one hid *The New Machiavelli* inside the chapel hymn-book, or read *Major Barbara* by flashlight under the bedclothes. To such ecstasies youth could add a passionate awareness of being alive, and--during the years 1914-1918--being alive by a miracle.

Looking back on those days I see that they had an epic quality, and that, after all, the school experiences of my generation were unique. Behind the murmur of genitive plurals in dusty classrooms and the plick-plock of cricket balls in the summer sunshine, there was always the rumble of guns, the guns that were destroying the world that Brookfield had made and that had made Brookfield. Sometimes these guns were actually audible, or we fancied they were; every weekday there was a rush to the newspapers, every Sunday a batch of names read out to stilled listeners. The careful assessments of schoolmasters were blotted out by larger and wilder markings; a boy who had been expelled returned as a hero with medals; those whose inability to conjugate *avoir* and *être* seemed likely in 1913 to imperil a career were to conquer France's enemies better than they did her language; offenders gated for cigarette-smoking in January were dropping bombs from the sky in December. It was a frantic world; and we knew it even if we did not talk about it. Slowly, inch by inch, the tide of war lapped to the gates of our seclusion; playing-fields were ploughed up for trenches and drill-grounds; cadet-corps duties took precedence over classroom studies; the school that had prepared so many beloved generations for life was preparing this one, equally beloved, for death.

When I said just now that I disliked military training and had no aptitude for it, I was putting the matter mildly. I dislike regimentation of any kind, and I loathe war, not only for its enthronement of the second-rate--in men, standards, and ideals. In the declension of spirit in which England fought, it is correct to say that we began with Rupert Brooke and ended with Horatio Bottomley. But at Brookfield the loftier mood prevailed even when it was no more than a cellophane illusion separating us from the visible darkness without.

On Sundays we attended Chapel and heard sermons that, as often as not, preached brotherly love and forgiveness of our enemies. On Mondays we watched cadets on the football-field bayoneting sacks with special aim for vital parts of the human body. This paradox did not, I am sure, affect most Brookfield boys as it did me. To be frank, it obsessed me; I would wonder endlessly whether Sunday's or Monday's behaviour were the more hypocritical. I have changed my attitude since. That Brookfield declined to rationalise warfare into its code of ethics while at the same time sending its sons to fight and die, seems to me now to have been pardonably illogical and creditably inconsistent; looking round on the present-day world of 1938, I can see that countries where high ideals are preached but not practised are at least better off than countries in which low ideals are both preached *and* practised.

Many of us at Brookfield, like myself, were too young--*just* too young--to see actual service in the War; yet during our last school years we lived under the shadow, for we knew or took for granted that if the War lasted we should be illogical and inconsistent in the same English way. Such tragic imminence hardly worried us, but it gave a certain sharpness to all the joys and a certain comfort for all the trivial hardships of school-life--gave also, in my own case, the clearest focus for memory. There is hardly a big event of those years that I do not associate with a Brookfield scene; Kitchener's death reminds me of cricketers hearing the news as they fastened pads in the pavilion; the Russian Revolution gives me the voice of a man, now dead, who talked about it instead of giving his usual geography lesson; the *Lusitania* sinking reminds me of early headlines, read hastily over a master's shoulder at breakfast. I composed a sonnet on the Russian Revolution, which my father had the temerity to send to Mr. A. G. Gardiner, eliciting from him the comment that it 'showed merit.' I also wrote a poem on the *Lusitania* which appeared in the *Cambridge Magazine,* a pacifist weekly run by Mr. C. K. Ogden, who has since distinguished himself by the invention of Basic English. These things I recount, not for vainglory (for they were not particularly good poems), but to reveal something of the mood of Brookfield, in which a boy could be eccentric enough to write poetry and subversive enough to write pacifist and revolutionary poetry without being either persecuted or ostracised. As a matter of fact, I was editor of the school magazine, and wrote for it articles, stories, and poems of all kinds and in all moods. Nobody tried to censor them; nobody tried to depose or harass me. Looking back on this genial indifference, it seems to me that Brookfield in wartime was not only less barbarian than the world outside it, but also less barbarian than many institutions in what we have since chosen to call peacetime. Is there a school in Soviet Russia where a student may offer even the mildest printed criticism of Stalin? Is there a debating society throughout all Nazi Germany that would dare to allow a Socialist to defend his faith? I suspect that nowadays the boys of Brookfield, members predominantly of the despised bourgeois capitalist class, are nevertheless free to be Marxian or Mosleyite if they like, and no doubt a few of them are writing wild stuff which in twenty years' time they will either forget or regret. Let us hope, however, that they will not forget the spirit of tolerance which today is in such grave peril because it is in the very nature of tolerance to take tolerance for granted.

I do not know whether this spirit obtained at other schools besides Brookfield. Probably at some it did and at others it didn't. But I stress it because the quality of any institution can be tested by the extent to which it withstands attack without compromising too much with the attacker. Granted that during the War all civilised institutions were subtly contaminated, which of them passed such a test most creditably? Perhaps we can say that England as a whole, though suffering vast changes, has survived more recognisably than any other country. She is more than the ghost of her former self--she has a good deal still left of the substance. Alone among the countries that participated substantially in the War, her national life is still reasonably well anchored. Mr. Chips, if he were alive (and I have reason to believe he is, in a few schools), could still give the same lessons as in 1908 (not an ideal educational programme, but one that at least attests the durability of a tradition), could still make the same jokes to a new generation that still understands them, could still offer himself in the kindly role of jester, critic, mentor, and friend. No upstart authority has yet compelled him to click his heels and begin the day with juju incantations of *Heils* and *Vivas*. He can still say, without fear of rubber truncheons: 'Umph . . . Mr. Neville Chamberlain . . . umph . . . I used to know his father when he was the wild man of Born--I mean Birmingham . . . but his sons have turned--umph--respectable. . . .'

This spirit of free criticism, even if it expresses itself no more momentously than as a classroom squib, is the sort of thing that makes English Conservatives liberal and keeps English Socialists conservative. It is the spirit that made Baldwin protest against Fascist brutality at the Albert Hall, that gives Citrine misgivings about Russia, and that united ninety per cent of Englishmen in fervent if soon-forgotten admiration of Dimitrov. It is the spirit that made Mr. Chips protest amidst the bomb explosions: 'These things that have mattered for a thousand years are not going to be snuffed out because some stink-merchant invents a new kind of mischief.'

Unfortunately, it looks as if they *are* going to be snuffed out. Mr. Chips was too valiant an optimist to face the tragic impasse of the twentieth century--the fact that civilisation, because in its higher manifestations it is essentially organised for peace, cannot long survive war--even a war supposedly undertaken on its behalf. There can be no war to end wars, because all wars begin other wars. There can be no such thing as a war to save democracy, because all wars destroy democracy. There could have been a peace to save what was left of democracy, but the chance of that came and went in 1919--the saddest year in all the martyrdom of man.

Here the reader may protest that much of the above arguments depends on the assumption that England and our institutions deserve to survive. There was a time when I would not by any means have taken this for granted. It was possible, then, to feel that the pre-War world, having encouraged or permitted a system that led to catastrophe, might as well be destroyed completely to make way for newer and better things. (It was possible, then, to say 'newer and better' as glibly as one says 'spick and span.') It was possible, then, to decry the public schools as the bulwark of a system that had had its day, to attack them for their creation of a class snobbery, to lampoon their play-the-game fetish and their sedate philistinism. That these attacks were partly justified one may as well admit. The public schools *do* create snobbery, or at any rate the illusion of superiority; you cannot train a ruling class without such an illusion. My point is that the English illusion has proved, on the whole, humaner and more endurable, even by its victims, than the current European illusions that are challenging and supplanting it; that the public-school Englishmen who flock to a Noel Coward revue to join in laughs against themselves are patterned better than the polychromed shirtwearers of the Continent who not only cannot laugh but dare not allow laughter. Granted that the long afternoon of English imperialism is over, that dusk is falling on a dominion wider if less solid than Rome's. Granted that the world is tired of us and our solar topees and our faded kip-lingerie, that it will not raise a finger to save us from eclipse. Time will bring regrets, if any. For myself, I do not object to being called a sentimentalist because I acknowledge the passing of a great age with something warmer than a sneer.

But the accusation of sentimentality comes oddly from those who extol the Russian collectivist as Rousseau extolled the noble savage. In some circles today it is even fashionable to decry the more literate occupations altogether and to redress the undoubted middle-class overweight in pre-War art by refusing hallmarks to anything modern

74

that cannot call itself 'proletarian.' This forces me to a confession (snobbish if you insist) that in my opinion a man need not be ashamed of having been educated--even at Brookfield and Cambridge. When I reflect on the manner in which the Gadarene pace of 1938 is being set by an ex-house-painter, I do not need to apologise for being an ex-public schoolboy (comic phrase though it is), and I can even turn with relief to the visionary ideals of a man whose reputation, faded today, will bloom again as we remember him more and more wistfully in the years ahead. And Woodrow Wilson was an ex-schoolmaster. Let history write the epitaph--England, liberalism, democracy were not so bad--not so good, either, on all occasions, but better, maybe, in a longer retrospect. Some of us may even survive to make such a retrospect. All over the world today the theme and accents of barbarism are being orchestrated, while the technique of mass-hypnotism, as practised by controlled press and radio, is being schooled to construct a façade of justification for any and every excess. The English illusion is dying; 'on dune and headland sinks the fire.' But there are other and fiercer fires. It is remarkable (if only a coincidence) that the first victims of the new ferocities have been countries in which there is a long tradition of cruelty (Chinese tortures, Ethiopian mutilations, Spanish bull-rings); one is almost tempted to a belief that the soil can be soured by ancestral lusts, and that English freedom from actual warfare within her own territories for two centuries has been, in effect, a cleansing and a purification. Perhaps this is too mystical for proof; perhaps it is just nonsense, anyway. But it is true that violence begets violence, that delight in the infliction of suffering is a poison in the bloodstream of nations as well as of individuals, and that soon we may be faced with the prospect of a world impelled to its doom by sadists and degenerates. In the next war (that is to say, in the war that has already begun) there will be no heroes charging splendidly to death because 'someone has blundered,' but grey-faced *morituri,* prone in their steel coffins, diving to kill and be killed because, in the reckoning of authority, no one has blundered at all.

Do not think I am blind to the faults of the age of which Mr. Chips and his type were the product as well as the makers. Its imperialism was, at its worst, smug, hypocritical, and predatory. Its *laissez-faire* capitalism resulted in such horrors as child-slavery in factories. Its vices were as solid as its virtues. But one fact does emerge from any critical analysis of the period beginning, roughly, with the Queen's accession and ending with her death--that it was possible, during this time, for an intelligent man in Western Europe to look around his world and believe that it was getting better. He could see the spread of freedom, in thought and creed and speech, and--even more important-- the spread of the belief that such an increase of freedom was an ultimate goal, even if it could not be immediately conceded. He could watch the transplantation of parliamentary government into lands where, though it might not wholly suit the soil, few doubted it would eventually flourish. He could believe that mechanical inventions were spreading civilisations because the chief mechanical invention of the time, the railway, was not (like the aeroplane) diabolically apt for use in warfare. He could observe each year new sunderings of barriers between lands until traveller and student could roam through Europe more freely than at any time since the break-up of Christendom.

True that the boy Dickens toiled in a blacking-factory, but he grew up free to scarify the system that had forced him to it; he had been a child-slave, but he was never a man-slave. True that Huxley was attacked for teaching that men and monkeys were somewhat the same; but he was never exiled for refusing to teach that Jews and Gentiles were altogether different. Scientists may have incurred the wrath of bishops for spreading what the latter considered to be evolutionary nonsense; they were never ordered by government to teach what every acknowledged authority considers to be Aryan nonsense. And while Karl Marx laboriously constructed his time-bomb to explode the bourgeoisie, his victims rewarded him with a ticket to the British Museum instead of a Leipzig trial, and a peaceful grave in Highgate Cemetery instead of a trench in front of a firing-squad.

Occasionally throughout the ages, the clouds of history show a rift and through it the sun of human betterment shines out for a few deceptive moments over a limited area. The Greece of Pericles was one such time and place; parts of China under certain dynasties offered the spectacle of another; Paraguay under the Jesuit Communists was perhaps a third. These few have little in common save a crust of security over the prevalent turbulence of mankind; the crust was thin and its promise of permanence false. But Victorian England sealed the volcano more stoutly than it had ever been sealed before, so that a man and his son and his son's son might live and die in the belief that the world would not witness certain things again. The crust, indeed, was such that even after the first shattering its debris is something to cling to--until the next.

All of which may sound a huge digression in a book dedicated to the memory of an old schoolmaster. But for me it is not so. I cannot think of my schooldays without the image of that incredible background--Zeppelins droning over sleeping villages, Latin lessons from which boys stepped into the brief lordliness of a second lieutenancy on the Somme. I cannot forget the little room where my friends and I fried sausages over a gas-ring and played George Robey records on the gramophone, and how, in that same little room with the sausages frying and the gramophone playing, one of us received a telegram with bad news in it, and how we all tried to sympathise, yet in the end arrived at no better idea than to open a hoarded tin of pineapple chunks to follow the sausages. I cannot forget cycling so often over the ridge of the Gogmagogs (which, as Mr. Chips always informed us, was the highest land between Brookfield and the Ural Mountains), and the soft fenland rain beginning to fall on Cambridge streets at dusk, with old men fumbling in and out of bookshops, and young men, spent after route-marches, scampering over ancient quadrangles. Those days were history, but most of us were too young to be historians, too young to disassociate the trivial from the momentous--gnarled desks and war-headlines, photogravure generals and the school butler who stood at the foot of the dormitory staircase and at lights-out warned sepulchrally--'Time, Gentlemen, Time.' It was Time in a way that so many of us could not realise. That warning marked the days during which, on an average, ten thousand men were killed.

Mr. Chips would walk between the lines of beds in the dormitory and turn out the lights. He was an old man then, and it was impossible to think he had ever been much younger. He seemed already ageless, beyond the reach of any time that could be called. Schooldays are a microcosm of life--the boy is born the day he enters the school and dies the day he leaves it; in between are youth, middle-age, and the elderly respectability of the sixth-form. But outside this cycle stands the schoolmaster, watching the three-year lifetimes as they pass him by, remembering faces and incidents as a god might remember history. An old schoolmaster, if he is well-liked and has dignity, is rather like a god. You can joke about him behind his back, but you must acknowledge him to his face while you love him a little carelessly in your hearts. This has been the relationship of good men and good gods since the world began.

There was no single schoolmaster I ever knew who was entirely Mr. Chips, but there were several who had certain of his attributes and achieved that best reward of a well-spent life--to grow old beloved. One of them was my father. He did not train aristocrats to govern the Empire or plutocrats to run their fathers' businesses, but he employed his wise and sweetening influence just as valuably among the thousands of elementary school boys who knew and know him still in a London suburb.

CHAPTER TWO

GERALD AND THE CANDIDATE

Gerald was eight when he first went to stay with Uncle Richard. He had no parents, and the frequent prep-school holidays had to be filled up somehow; that was the reason. He was a quiet boy, full of dreams. For weeks during the winter term at Grayshott (which was the prep school for Brookfield) he had talked to Martin Secundus about the visit: 'I say, Martin, I'll have to go into training--Uncle Richard always takes people such long walks when they go and stay with him. He's a great explorer, you know. Once he was nearly killed in the jungle by a tiger. He can climb any mountain there is. And he lives in an old castle with a moat round it, and before you can get in you have to give the password.'

Actually Gerald had never seen Uncle Richard or where he lived. Everything was new to him--the house and the town and the kind of country, the journey there in the train that went 'You-can-if-you-like--You-can-if-you-like,' and not just 'No, you mustn't--No, you mustn't,' like the local train to Grayshott; and the first meeting at twilight on Browdley station platform with Uncle Richard. The platform was made of wooden planks, and as Gerald walked along it the thump, thump, thump made him think of his second favourite 'pretend'--that he was a great general, marching at the head of soldiers--'Follow me, my men!' But he was soon back at his chief and almost permanent 'pretend'--that he was the engine-driver of the Scotch express, which was half an hour late with the King and Queen on board, and the King had said to the station-master: 'My good fellow, I *must* arrive in time,' and the stationmaster had answered: 'Well, your Majesty, that's going to be a difficult matter, but we have one man, Gerald Holloway, whom we can try. If anyone can get you there, he will.' Steadily, steadily, throughout the night, a hand always on the throttle-lever, eyes peering ahead . . . that was how it went on. Very often the King knighted him as the station clock struck the hour at which the train was due to arrive.

But this time Gerald hadn't a chance to think as far as that, because of Uncle Richard.

'Well, my boy,' said Uncle Richard, in a very loud, gruff voice. Then he arranged with a porter about having Gerald's trunk and tuck-box sent on, and after that began to walk away towards the ticket-barrier. Gerald was sorry to be whisked off the platform so soon; he rather wanted to look at the engine--it was a Four-Four-Nought. None of the grown-up people he knew had any idea what a Four-Four-Nought was; but Gerald considered it quite everyday knowledge.

'So you're Gerald,' said Uncle Richard, when they came to the street.

Gerald said he was.

'You'll have to speak up a bit, my boy--I'm a little deaf. Gerald, eh? Well, you've come here at a lively time, and no mistake.' And he made a noise in his throat which Gerald thought was like something, if he could only think what. It sounded like 'wuff-wuff.' 'Yes, a right-down lively time. Better make a good start, young shaver, and wear your colours.'

Whereat Uncle Richard halted under a lamp and fished in his pocket, producing after some search a large red rosette which he stooped and pinned to the lapel of Gerald's overcoat. Gerald looked up at him with an interest that suddenly quickened to excitement. Was it possible that here, at last, was a grown-up who knew the things that really mattered in the world? From that moment, at any rate, he was aware that Uncle Richard was not to be classed with any other people. He smiled, privately to himself, and then with open friendliness at the big face that overtopped his own.

'There you are, my boy. Red's for Liberal. Consequently is, the folks'll know what you are.'

Gerald did not understand this at all, but he was quite contented as he trotted along. He knew he was going to like Uncle Richard.

Uncle Richard lived at Number 2, The Parade, which was the best house in Browdley's best street--a double preeminence signalised by the fact that none of the other streets in Browdley had front gardens, and none of the other front gardens in the Parade was as big as Uncle Richard's. His, indeed, was about the size of a railway waiting-room, and nothing grew in it except some evergreens that were really ever-black. Nevertheless, the social gulf proclaimed by them and by their cindery soil was immense. They made the Parade the Park Lane of Browdley. Uncle Richard's was the end house of a row of twelve--grimy, bay-windowed, and ornamented in the most florid mid-Victorian style; and Browdley, in point of fact, was just a Northern industrial town of some eight or ten thousand inhabitants, mostly employed in the local industries of iron-founding and calico-printing. In the junior geography form at Grayshott, noisy with talk of capes and bays and county towns and what belonged to whom, the word 'Browdley' was unknown. It was the sort of place that nobody ever went to and that nobody had ever heard of.

But that, if he had known anything about it when he was eight, would have seemed to Gerald just a part of the vast grown-up conspiracy to avoid seeing things as they really were. As he and Uncle Richard walked through the streets from the station to the Parade, he was quite sure about Browdley and equally sure about himself in it. With that red rosette in his coat-lapel he was a knight, flaunting his banner and about to do something heroic; and Uncle Richard was clearly another knight; and Browdley was the beautiful and mysterious place where they both had to do whatever it was. The streets of that magic city were glittering with bright windows, and Gerald's eyes, as he walked along, could just peer over the sills and sometimes under the drawn blinds. Wonderful sights--an old man leaning over a fire; a woman peeling potatoes at a table covered with dishes; a little girl sitting on a high stool in front of a piano. Such people might have been seen elsewhere, but they would not have been the same; and that was because he was with Uncle Richard and they were both wearing those red rosettes.

Soon they came to the house. It had a street lamp outside it that shone a green light, and whenever afterwards Gerald mentioned this and Aunt Lavinia said (as she sometimes did): 'What nonsense, Gerald! Did anyone ever see a street lamp with a green light!'--Gerald used to reply: 'Well, it *was* a green light, and it made the house look wonderful. And there was a dragon on the front door.' Whereupon Aunt Lavinia would usually say: 'Don't take any notice of him, Mrs. So-and-so. He *romances.'* But there *was* this green light, and the dragon on the front door was the brass knocker, which seemed to Gerald exactly like a dragon.

Uncle Richard unlocked the door with a key and guided Gerald down a dark passage-way, along which there were other doors with strips of light under them, and the sound of voices beyond. Suddenly

Uncle Richard opened one. 'Well, here's the young criminal!' he said, weighing his hand down on Gerald's shoulder.

Then Gerald looked up and saw what a huge, red face his uncle had, and how hair grew in tufts out of his nose and ears, how thick his fingers were, and how, when he spoke, the light in the room seemed to blink. And then suddenly he knew what the 'wuff-wuff' was really like--it was like the bark of a big black dog. 'Well, well, here we are, my boy. This is your Aunt Flo. She'll get you a bite of supper, and then off you go to bed.'

Gerald was rather dashed at that; surely bed could not be part of this new and marvellous existence? But Aunt Flo, who wore glasses, smiled and patted his cheek. 'You look tired after your journey,' she said, but Gerald, who felt anything but tired, did not reply. Then she shouted to Uncle Richard: 'He says he's tired after his journey'; which was really not true at all. By that time, however, Gerald was staring round the room and at everything in it. It was a very warm red room, with a crackling fire and a brass rail stretching the whole length of the mantelpiece over the fireplace. To one side stood a long dresser, scrubbed white, and on this there was a queer, dome-shaped object covered with a dark cloth. 'That's Polly,' said Aunt Flo. 'She's gone to bed now and we mustn't wake her. A parrot, Gerald--have you never seen a parrot before?'

Of course he had; he had been to the Zoo. 'Does it talk?' he asked.

'Yes, she can say "Give me a nut." You'll see tomorrow.'

Gerald was a little awed at the prospect of seeing Polly, though he didn't think 'Give me a nut' was much of a thing to say, even for a parrot. Then he noticed that the room had two windows, only one of which had a blind drawn over it; the other looked through into another sort of room. Now this was a peculiar thing--so peculiar that he could not help being rude (for Aunt Lavinia had always assured him that it was rude to ask questions). 'Where does that lead to, Uncle Richard?' he said.

'He wants to know what's out there!' shouted Aunt Flo.

'Out there, my boy? Wuff-wuff. Why, that's the greenhouse. Only we don't use it as a greenhouse now. It's where I keep my tricycle.'

'Tricycle?'

'Never seen a tricycle?'

'I've seen a parrot, but I've never seen a tricycle,' answered Gerald; so Uncle Richard beckoned him nearer to the window, and there it was, quite plainly--a tricycle. And on the handlebars, as on the lapels of Gerald's and Uncle Richard's coats, there was a red rosette.

Gerald went to bed that night in a whirl of excitement that made him forget to be frightened because of the dark. Once he heard a lot of talking downstairs and Uncle Richard wuff-wuffing in the passage. Then he closed his eyes and thought of Polly and the tricycle, and the King walked up to the engine-cab and said: 'Rise, Sir Gerald,' and pinned on his coat the biggest red rosette in the world.

In the morning, that first morning at Uncle Richard's, Gerald awoke with a half-fear that it would all be different. But no; when he came downstairs, Uncle Richard was there, looking just as big in the daylight. 'Good morning,' he began. 'I hope you slept with your colours pinned on to your night-shirt.' Now this was exactly what Gerald had done, but he had not been going to tell anybody. Marvellous that Uncle Richard should have guessed! 'Yes, of course,' answered Gerald, and Uncle Richard laughed loudly and then went to look at something on the wall and blew his nose like a trumpet. 'Glass is rising-- consequently is, my boy, we'll have some fine days for you.'

All at once Gerald looked across the room and saw Polly. She was perched inside the cage on a wooden bar, with her head cocked sideways as if she were listening carefully. Oh, what a beautiful parrot! He ran towards her and she began to squawk and ruffle her feathers, which were bright green, with little patches of red and yellow. 'Don't frighten Polly,' said Aunt Flo. 'When she gets to know you she'll let you stroke her, but don't try yet--she might nip.' Gerald felt cross at being squawked at; after all, he had only meant to be friendly. So, when Aunt Flo and Uncle Richard were both looking away, he took a pencil out of his pocket and pushed it through the bars of the cage. This made the bird squawk more than ever, but Gerald had time to withdraw and hide the pencil before anyone saw him.

'Now that's very naughty of Polly,' said Aunt Flo, coming over and putting her head against the cage. 'Gerald's come to see you and you're being very rude, so you shall just go back to bed again.' And she grabbed the piece of dark cloth and pulled it down over the cage. 'She deserves it,' Aunt Flo added, 'for being in such a bad humour.'

Nobody ever knew that Gerald had poked the parrot with a pencil. It was a secret for as long as the world should last.

There was porridge and a brown egg for breakfast, and afterwards a girl came into the room. Uncle Richard said: 'Aha, the gathering of the clans. We must introduce you . . . Olive . . . and Gerald . . . We're going to put you to work this morning--both of you.'

She looked about the same age as Gerald and had straight yellow hair and blue eyes. He did not like girls as a rule, but he noticed that she was wearing the same kind of red rosette, and immediately he saw what it all meant in a flash--it was a secret society, and they were all sworn to help one another, even girls. So he said politely: 'Hello.'

Then Uncle Richard told them what he wanted them both to do. It was a grand adventure. They had to walk along the neighbouring streets and put a red bill through every letter-box, giving a double-knock afterwards, like a postman. Gerald had often practised being a postman, so he was overjoyed. If a house hadn't got a letter-box, then they would have to push the bill under the front door. It was all most important work, and they must wear their red rosettes all the time.

So they went out with the bills and began along the Parade. How beautiful the Parade was in the lovely sunshine! Some people asked them inside the houses and gave them sweets and pennies, which only proved to Gerald that real life wasn't a bit like the silly make-believe of being at school. And some day, when he left Grayshott, there would be real life all the time. He was so busy knocking like a postman that he hardly spoke to Olive, except once, when a whistle in the distance reminded him to ask: 'Have you ever been faster than sixty miles an hour?'

'We have a horse that can run as fast as that,' said Olive.

'A horse as fast as a train?' echoed Gerald scornfully, but he was a little perturbed as well. He just answered, very off-hand: 'Oh, a race-horse--that doesn't count'--and let the conversation lapse.

When they had finished giving out the bills they went back to Uncle Richard's, and there another odd thing happened. A very old lady was in the passage-way talking to Uncle Richard and Aunt Flo, and as Gerald and Olive came in she lifted her spotty veil and stared. 'Yours?' she said, and Aunt Flo shouted: 'She's asking who they belong to, Richard!' Uncle Richard answered: 'My nephew, this is--wuff-wuff--and this'--pointing to Olive--'is the Candidate's little girl.'

That was the first time that Gerald ever heard of the Candidate.

The Browdley by-election was what the newspapers called 'closely contested.' Sir Thomas Barton, a cotton magnate, was opposed by Mr. Courtenay Beale, a young London barrister with a superfluity of brains and bounce. Sir Thomas, wealthy, middle-aged, and a widower, liked to play the democrat on these occasions; and as, in any case, there were no good hotels in Browdley, he found it convenient to lodge with Uncle Richard during the campaign. In another sense, of course, he found it highly inconvenient; Number 2, The Parade, seemed a strange habitation after his baronial mansion a hundred miles away. In his own mind he saw Uncle Richard's house as 'just an ordinary small house in a row'--he totally failed to perceive the immense social significance of the front garden. And Uncle Richard himself he thought a decent, well-meaning fellow, with some local influence, no doubt--a retired tradesman, wasn't he?--something of the sort. His wife, too, a good woman--fortunately, too, a good cook. Everything spotlessly clean, of course. And no children--only a little boy staying with them, a neph-ew--very quiet--one hardly knew he was there. Useful, too, as a playmate for Olive.

All this was remote from the world that Gerald lived in, and how-ever much he probed it by questioning he could not really make it his own.

'Uncle Richard, what is a Candidate?'

'He wants to know who the Candidate is, Richard!'

'Oho--taking an interest in politics already, eh? Wuff-wuff! Why, he's a Liberal--that's why we're trying to get him in.'

'Get in where?'

'He wants to know all about him, Richard, I do believe!'

'You mean his name? Well, my boy, he's called Sir Thomas Barton. Do you know what "Sir" means?'

This time it was Gerald's turn to shout. 'Yes, it means he's a knight.'

'Right to a T, my boy. Knighted by the King--consequently is, you have to call him "Sir." Be careful of that, mind, if you should ever happen to meet him on the stairs.'

All of which was tremendous confirmation of something that Ger-ald had long suspected--that he and Uncle Richard were real people, knowing real things. A knight, indeed! And on the stairs! That was how you were liable to meet knights, but no grown-up except Uncle Richard had ever seemed to realise it.

'You see,' added Uncle Richard, pointing along the passage towards the always closed door of the front parlour, 'that's *his* room. Never you go making a noise outside of it, because you might disturb him when he's at work.'

'At work?'

'Yes, my goodness, and plenty of it. Didn't I tell you, my boy, he's trying to Get In? And you and me and your Aunt have all got to help him, otherwise the Other Candidate'll Get In!'

This was the first time that Gerald had ever heard of the Other Candidate.

Marvellous, mysterious days. Every morning when he came down-stairs Gerald found Uncle Richard still up, and every night when he went to bed Uncle Richard was still down. Was it possible that he never had to go to bed at all? And every morning he tapped the barometer (Gerald knew all about that now) and made some queer remark that was supposed to be funny; at any rate, it made Uncle Richard himself laugh. One morning he said: 'Fine day for the race,' and Gerald pricked up his ears and said: 'What race?'

Then Uncle Richard's face crinkled up suddenly. 'The human race,' he answered. He went on laughing at that until Aunt Flo said: 'Come and have some breakfast and stop plaguing the boy.'

But Gerald wasn't plagued at all. He smiled at Uncle Richard to show that he appreciated the joke, whatever it was, and that, anyhow, he and Uncle Richard were on the same side in the great battle.

The joy of being sure of this sharpened the joy of giving out bills and knocking at doors; there was also a song that the boys from the streets round about would sing:

> *'A Li-ber-al Tom Barton is,*
> *And Li-ber-als are we,*
> *We'll vote for Barton, all of us,*
> *And make him our M.P.'*

Gerald liked this because he knew the tune (it was 'Auld Lang Syne'), but he couldn't understand all the words. However, the words of songs never mattered. But he did know that 'Tom Barton' was really wrong, so he always sang 'Sir Thomas,' very quietly to himself, so that he should be right without anyone hearing him.

(And afterwards, when the Candidate had Got In, he would tell people that he owed it all to one person--someone who had helped him by handing out bills, and who had called him by his proper name all the time; moreover, he had a most important engagement in London, and though there was a special train with steam up waiting for him at Browdley station, no one would undertake to drive it fast enough to reach London in time. So Gerald cried out: '*I* will, Sir Thomas . . .' and Uncle Richard waved to him from the platform, as the huge engine--a Pacific Four-Six-Two, by the way--gathered speed . . .)

'Is the Other Candidate a knight?' he once asked Uncle Richard.

'Eh, what's that? Wuff-wuff--young Beale a knight? God bless my soul, no. A little jumped-up carpet-bagger, that's all *he* is.'

The strangest things were happening all the time in that enchanted city of Browdley. Houses were decked with blue and red flags (blue, Gerald learned, was the Other Candidate's colour); windows were full of bills and cards; at every street corner in the evenings groups of people gathered, and sometimes a man got up and shouted at them, waving his arms about. Excitement filled the marketplace and ran along the streets; the little brown houses, doors wide open on to the pavements, were alive with eagerness and gossip and the knowledge of something about to happen. Gerald, walking about with Uncle Richard, could sniff the battle of Good and Evil in the air.

'Well, Dick. D'ye think he'll get in?'

'We're doing our best, Tom.'

'It'll be a touch-and-go with him, anyway. T'other Candidate's gaining ground.'

'A carpet-bagger, Tom, if ever there was one--a carpet-bagger.'

'They do say he's got one o' them motorcars.'

'He *would* have. Anything to make a noise.'

In the morning the rumour was confirmed. The Other Candidate had a motor-car, and it was one of the very first motor-cars to appear in most of the streets of Browdley. Gerald, in secret, would not have minded looking at it; but because it belonged to the Other Candidate he pictured himself driving an express train and overtaking it, along a parallel road, so quickly that he could hardly see it at all. But, no, perhaps that was too easy. He was riding Uncle Richard's tricycle instead, and even *that* overtook it. And the Other Candidate scowled and shouted after him: 'Who will rid me' (like Henry II and Thomas à Becket in the history book) 'of this turbulent young man who rides a tricycle so fast that I cannot catch him up in my motor-car?' (Eight knights sprang forward and ran after Gerald, but they could not catch him.)

Actually Gerald spent most of his time in the streets near Uncle Richard's house. Sometimes, if it were raining, he played in the greenhouse; there were red and blue panes of glass in the greenhouse door. If you looked through the red, everything was hot and stormy; if you looked through the blue, it was like night-time. That was very wonderful.

One day he had a tremendous adventure. Browdley lies in a valley, and beyond the town, steepening as it rises, there is a green-brown lazy-looking mountain called Mickle. A few scattered farms occupy the lower slopes, and at one of these, Jones's Farm, it had been arranged that Gerald and Olive should leave some bills. A pony-cart drew up outside Uncle Richard's house soon after breakfast, and the journey began at a steady trot through street after street that Gerald had never been in before. The horse swished its tail from side to side, waving a red rosette tied on to it; big posters decorated the cart. The man who drove was called Fred. It was a lovely blue sunshiny morning, and when they had climbed a little way and looked back, they could see all Browdley flat below them, covered with a thin smoke-cloud, the factory chimneys sticking out of it like pins in a pincushion. Above them, very big now, the mountain lifted up. Gerald had never been close to a mountain before. He felt madly happy. The lane narrowed to a stony track where Fred had to get down several times to open gates. At last they reached the farmhouse where Mrs. Jones lived. She was standing at the doorway wiping her arms on an apron and smiling at them; she was very fat and had hair piled up on top of her head. When Gerald and Olive got down from the cart she hugged them. 'Well . . . well . . . well . . .' she began, leading them inside the house; and just as they got into the kitchen a tabby cat suddenly moved from the hearthrug towards Gerald, tail erect. Gerald loved cats and stooped to stroke it, but he hadn't to stoop far, because (so the thought came to him) the cat was quite as large as a dog. Then he reflected that that wasn't a very sensible comparison, because dogs could be of all sizes, whereas cats had only one size, whatever size they were. Was that the way to put it? Anyway, Mrs. Jones's cat was a monster. It lifted up its head and met his hand in a warm, eager pressure that was beautiful to him. 'Isn't she a big pussy?' said Mrs. Jones, standing with her fists at 'hips firm,' as they called it at Grayshott.

'She's a big cat,' said Gerald gravely.

'Her name's Nib,' continued Mrs. Jones, and began to say 'Nibby, Nibby, Nibby,' in a high-pitched voice. But the cat, after one shrewd upward glance, knew that this was all nonsense, and continued to heave up to Gerald's hand. While Gerald was thus entranced, Olive remembered the bills they had brought and handed them over. 'Lawksa-mussy,' said Mrs. Jones, glancing at them, 'it's Jones as'll read these, not me. A Liberal 'e is, that's very sure, even if it was his dyin' day.'

Then she waddled away to a farther room, the cat abruptly following her, and presently returned with pieces of cake, glasses, and a jug. 'Nettle-drink,' she said. The cat was purring loudly. 'Sup it up--it'll do you good.'

Gerald was looking at the mountain through the doorway. In the sunlight it looked as if it were moving towards him.

'Is it the highest mountain in England?' he asked.

'Nay, that I can't say for certain--it'll happen not be as high as some on 'em.'

'Isn't it the highest mountain of anywhere?' asked Gerald desperately; but neither Mrs. Jones nor Fred seemed to understand. Fred said: "Tis only Mickle--I wouldn't call it much of a mountain at all.'

GERALD AND THE CANDIDATE

All at once Gerald realised that it didn't matter how they answered: it *was* the highest mountain, the highest in the world, and he was going to climb it, like the men in the snowstorm in his geography book.

He put down his glass and walked to the doorway. 'I'm going up there,' he said.

'Nay, you can't, you'd get lost on Mickle,' said Mrs. Jones.

'But I want to see what's over the other side,' Gerald went on.

'Take 'em both up, Fred, if they want,' Mrs. Jones then said. 'It'll be a bit o' fresh air for 'em.'

Fred nodded and began to trudge slowly up the steep track, Gerald and Olive following. But after a little while Gerald scampered ahead, because he liked to think that nobody had ever climbed the mountain before. It was a dangerous thing to do, and only he, the famous mountaineer and engine-driver, dare risk it. Up, up, scrambling through bracken and heather; there were tigers, too, that you had to watch out for. His blood was racing as he reached the smooth green summit. The earth was at his feet, the whole earth, and over the other side, which he had been so curious about, a further mountain was to be seen-- doubtless the second highest mountain in the world. Far below he could make out the tower of Browdley Church, with a tramcar crawling beside it like a red beetle.

Suddenly he saw a halfpenny lying on the ground. 'Look what I've found!' he cried, triumphantly; then he lay down in the cool blue air and waited for the others to come up.

Fred smoked in silence while Gerald talked to Olive.

'What makes your father a Candidate?'

'Because there's an election.'

'But what's that?'

'It means he has to get in.'

'Where does he get in?'

'In the house.'

'Can't anybody get in?'

'Only if you're a Candidate.'

'Does he ever have a special train?'

'A special train? I--I don't know.'

'Don't know what a special train is? Do you like trains? When I came here there was a Four-Four-Nought on our train. Bet you don't know what that means.'

No answer.

'Are you afraid to touch a snail?'

'No. And I'm not afraid to touch a bee, either. Even a bumble-bee. I don't suppose you've ever seen a bumble-bee.'

'Oh yes, I have. It's like a piece of flying cat. I wouldn't be afraid to touch one. But I'll bet you'd be afraid to stand on the edge of the platform while the Scotch express dashed through at sixty miles an hour. I did that once. I stood right on the edge.'

'Why?'

'It was a test. None of the others could do it. My father couldn't. Or Uncle Richard. Even the stationmaster couldn't.'

'Why not?'

'Because the train was going too fast. It was really going at eighty miles an hour, not sixty.'

Then there was a long silence, while Gerald lay back staring at the sky. He was very, very happy.

When you are a child, everything you think and dream of has a piercing realness that never happens again; there is no blurred background to that stereoscopic clarity, no dim perspective to drag at the heart's desire. That little world you live in is the widest, the loveliest, and the sweetest; it can be the bitterest also.

To Gerald, alone in his own vivid privacy, everything seemed miraculously right except the Other Candidate, who was miraculously wrong. The warm red room with the brass rail over the fireplace, and the greenhouse with the tricycle in it, and the parrot who never forgave him and whom he never forgave, were part of a secret intimacy in which Uncle Richard and Olive and Aunt Flo were partners (in descending order of importance), and over which, only a little lower than the angels, loomed the Candidate. Gerald could never catch a glimpse of the Candidate, though, after Uncle Richard's hint, he always looked out for him on the stairs. He knew that the Candidate lived in Uncle Richard's house, working in the front parlour with the door always closed, and sleeping in the front bedroom over it; yet he could never (and it must have been pure chance) see him entering or leaving the house, or passing from one room to another. Partly, of course, this was because of Aunt Flo's continual fidgeting. 'Mind now, Gerald, be very quiet, and no playing in the passage--the Candidate'll be in any minute.' Or: 'Gerald, time for bed now--must have you out of the way before the Candidate comes in!' Long after she had put him to bed and turned out the light, Gerald would he awake, thinking and listening; often he *heard* the Candidate, but it was never any words--just the mix-up of footsteps and talk. Once he said to Uncle Richard: 'Can't I ever *see* the Candidate?'--and Uncle Richard answered: 'Not now, my boy--he's far too busy. But I'll take you out tonight and you'll see him then.'

So that night Uncle Richard took Gerald to the market-place, which was full of a great crowd of people. Uncle Richard hoisted him on to his shoulder so that he could see; and far away, over all the cloth caps, a man was standing on a cart and shouting something. Gerald could not hear what it was he was shouting, because people round about were shouting much louder. 'Aha, we're in good time,' said Uncle Richard, in Gerald's ear. 'That's only old Burstall--don't you take any notice of *him*. He'll only go on till the Candidate comes, that's all. Watch out--you'll soon see the Candidate!'

The talking and shouting went on, and Gerald, perched on Uncle Richard's shoulder, began to feel very sleepy. Everyone seemed to be smoking pipes and cigarettes, and the smoke rose in a cloud and got into his eyes, so that it became hard to keep them open. The man on the cart continued to talk, but he wasn't interesting either to watch or listen to . . . and still the Candidate didn't come. . . . Then suddenly, with a jerk, Gerald felt himself being lowered to the ground and Uncle Richard was stooping and shaking him. All around were the legs of people hurrying past. 'Why,' exclaimed Uncle Richard, 'I do believe you've been asleep! Didn't you see the Candidate?'

Then Gerald realised what had happened. Uncle Richard laughed heartily. 'Well, I don't know--you are a rum fellow, and no mistake! Badgering me all the time to see him, and then when he does come you drop off to sleep!'

'I couldn't help it,' answered Gerald miserably. 'I didn't know. . . . Why didn't you nudge me?'

'Nudge you? God bless my soul, I thought you were wide awake!' Uncle Richard went on laughing as if it were a great joke instead of something very sad. 'Well, my boy, you missed something good, I can tell you. The Candidate's a treat--a fair treat!'

Days went by, and the chance did not come again. All the commotion of shouting and singing and waving red rosettes was reaching some kind of climax that Gerald, even without understanding it, could clearly sense; every morning the magic was renewed, and Uncle Richard tapped the barometer with more zest for the day ahead.

In Gerald the desire to see the Candidate had grown into a great longing. It coloured all Browdley in a glow of excitement, for, as Uncle Richard had said: 'You'll see him, my boy, if you keep your eyes open! Ha, ha--if you keep your eyes open, eh? That hits the mark, eh? Wuff-wuff. . . . He's everywhere in Browdley--you're bound to see him. But mind, now, no hanging about the passage--that would only annoy him. He's putting up a hard fight--we've all got to help.'

That was so, of course, and it was for that reason he and Olive kept on putting bills in letter-boxes. It was like the Secret Service, where you did things you didn't properly understand because the King ordered you to; though you never really saw the King till afterwards, when the danger was all past and he received you at the Palace and conferred on you the Most Noble and Distinguished Order of the Red Rosette.

So Gerald wandered about, eager and happy and preoccupied, full of thoughts of his mission and stirred by wild hopes that some time, any time, on the stairs or at the corner of the street, the Candidate might suddenly appear. A vision! It was terribly exciting to think of-- quite the most exciting thing since Martin Secundus had measles and went to the sanatorium, and Gerald used to wait about outside thinking that Martin would probably die and would want to give him a last message from his death-bed.

One afternoon Gerald was alone in the house, reading the Yearly Report of the Browdley and District Friendly and Cooperative Society, which he had found under the cushion of a chair, and which seemed to him, for the moment, of engrossing interest. There was a picture in it of the first train entering Browdley station in 1853, and beside it, a picture of the first shop opened by the Browdley and District Friendly and Cooperative Society in the same year. A long, long time ago, before Uncle Richard was born. Gerald began to think about a long, long time ago, but it was hard to think like that. He was relieved when the tinkle of a bell in the street outside reminded him of his unique position--he was alone in the house, and the bell belonged to the ice-cream cart that visited the Parade every afternoon. Gerald had a passion for ice-cream, and one of his constant puzzlements was that grownups, who had pockets full of money and complete freedom to do anything they liked, didn't eat ice-cream all day long. Aunt Flo, for example, would nibble at a spoonful and say she 'didn't care for it much--it's too cold' (what a ridiculous thing to say!) and Uncle Richard wouldn't have any at all. Profound mystery of human behaviour! Sometimes, however, they had allowed Gerald to go out into the street with a cup and buy a halfpennyworth. Now, with a sudden consciousness of his great chance, Gerald reached down from the dresser the largest cup he could find and took two pennies carefully out of his purse. Then he ran down the passage and out at the front door. The ice-cream cart, drawn by a little donkey, stood in the middle of the roadway, with the ice-cream man sitting perched up inside it. It was a beautiful cart, covered with coloured pictures and gilt lettering, and with four bright brass pillars holding up a flat roof. It made the ice-cream man, whose name was Ulio, look like a king on his throne. 'Two-pennyworth,' said Gerald, a little nervously, lest Mr. Ulio should see into his inmost heart. But Mr. Ulio just jabbed at his ice-cream and scooped a few slices into the cup--and not very much more, Gerald thought, than he had formerly got for a halfpenny.

Gerald ran back into the house and began to eat the ice-cream in a great hurry, because it was 'waste' when it melted, and it always did, towards the bottom of the cup. The parrot squawked and pattered up and down the bars of the cage; she always demanded a share of anything that people were eating. Gerald, however, took no notice of her, partly because of their long-standing feud, but chiefly because he would not have given away even a fraction of his ice-cream to anybody. While he was eating ice-cream he was transfixed with greed; mind and body were united in the fulfillment of desire.

When the cup was empty he became his more usual self again; his passions became more mystical, more closely intertwined with thought. He was not sure what he would do next, but he ran into the greenhouse and stared for a time through the blue glass, which he liked better than the red. He was excitingly alone. The Candidate was out, Uncle Richard was out on his tricycle, Olive and Aunt Flo were 'round the corner' on some errand. Suddenly a knock came at the front door and Gerald ran back to open it, hoping beyond hope that the Candidate might have returned unexpectedly and that he would say, when they had shaken hands: 'Gerald, in all Browdley you are the man I have most of all been wanting to meet. I have heard of you, of course. Come into my parlour and let us talk. Has Mr. Ulio gone out of the street? I hope not, for I should like you to join me in a large dish of his excellent ice-cream. . . .' But no; it was an ordinary man, just an ordinary man, wanting to see the Candidate. Gerald said he was out.

'Hasn't he come back yet? There's this letter for him. He's been up at the farms on Mickle this morning, so they say, but I reckoned he'd be back by now. Will you give him this letter when he comes?'

'Is it very important?'

'Oh, no, it'll do when he has a minute to spare. No particular hurry.'

Gerald gave his promise, but as soon as the man was gone he came to the conclusion that the letter *was* very important, and that the man had only said it wasn't because it really was. Secret Service people did things like that. And since it was very important, and if the Candidate were still at the farms on Mickle, why should not Gerald go up there himself, immediately, and deliver it to the Candidate in person? They would meet, perhaps, in Mrs. Jones's kitchen. 'Where is the young man who brought this message? He has saved my life. *What?* He lives with Uncle Richard? And I never knew it! How can I ever forgive myself! . . . Mrs. Jones, bring us some of your nettle-drink--we will all quaff together.'

Gerald left the house, walked to the centre of the town, crossed the market-place, and took the turning up the hill. The day was not so fine as when he had set out for Mickle before, and the mountain itself looked heavy and dark; but Gerald did not mind that--he had too many exciting thoughts. At one place where the street narrowed and two factories faced each other, he imagined that the walls were leaning over, and that if he didn't hurry they would fall on him. So he broke into a scamper till the danger was past, and then stood panting and not quite sure whether he was really afraid or only pretending. Then he took the Candidate's letter out of his pocket and looked at it solemnly; it reminded him of what he had to do. He hurried on. Presently he came to the end of the houses; the lane twisted and became steeper; a few drops of rain fell. He thought of the warm red room at Uncle Richard's with Aunt Flo making potato-cakes as she probably would be by this time, and just beginning to wonder where he was; the clatter of cups and the kettle singing, the parrot squawking for a spoonful of tea. Would it not be safer to go back? But no; no; he must climb up and up and deliver the letter to the Candidate. He came to a line of high trees; if there were an odd number of them, perhaps he would go back, but if there were an even number he would keep on. There were twelve. He often settled difficult problems by this kind of method, though he never told anybody about it, except Martin Secundus, who understood. He began to walk faster uphill. You cannot do it, they all cried, mocking him as he passed by; it is too dangerous to climb this mountain; no one has ever done it and come back alive. It is my duty, he answered proudly, as he swept on.

Then he began to see that the sky was darkening, not with rain only, but with twilight; the top of Mickle lay in a little cloud, as if someone had drawn the outline of the mountain in ink and then smudged it. He felt tired and his legs trembled. Soon the rain began to fall faster, until there was no mountain to see at all--only a grey curtain covering it; but he knew he was on the right path, because of the steepness. Never, remarked the famous engine-driver, do I remember such a night of wind and rain. . . .

94

He walked on and on, climbing all the time, till the rain had soaked through all his clothes, and was clammy-cold against his skin.

Suddenly he heard a noise, a strange noise, a kind of rumbling and muttering from the road ahead. He stopped, scared a little, listening to it above the swishing of the rain and the whine of the wind in the telegraph-wires. The noise grew louder, and all at once two bright yellow lights poked round a corner and came rushing at him. He ran for safety to the side of the road, and there slipped on some mud and fell. The next he knew was that the rumbling noise had halted somehow beside him, and had changed and lowered its key. Someone was holding him up and feeling his arms.

'No bones broken, Roberts. I'm sure we didn't touch him--he just slipped and fell over. We'd best take him along with us, anyhow.'

'Yes, sir.'

Gerald found himself lifted off his feet with his face pressing against something rain-drenched and fluffy. A ray of yellow light caught it, and he saw then that it was a rosette fastened to a man's overcoat.

A blue rosette.

Blue.

Once again the truth besieged him in an overpowering rush. This man who was holding him must be the Other Candidate . . . and the noise-making Thing nearby must be the motor-car. There could be no doubt about it. And he was shaken. He felt fear, horror, and the simple presence of evil. 'Let me go!' he shouted desperately, wriggling and twisting and hitting the man's face with his fists.

'Here, what's the matter, youngster?'

'Let me go--let me go!'

'What's all the fuss about? You aren't hurt, are you? Better get him in the car, Roberts.'

'No! No, no!'

'Well, what the devil *do* you want?'

Now that the man had used a swear, like that, Gerald was more certain than ever that he must be the Other Candidate. And knowing that he was the Other Candidate, it was easy to see what a wicked face he had. Terrible eyes and a curving nose and a sneery mouth, like pictures of pirates. And what he wanted to do, undoubtedly, was to steal the Candidate's letter that Gerald was carrying. Gerald looked around wildly. The man had put him down to earth again, that was something; but both the men seemed so huge above him, and the falling rain seemed to enclose the darkness through which lay his only chance of escape.

'Come on,' said the man roughly. 'This is no place to hang about all night. We'd better make sure and take him along with us, Roberts.'

'Very good, sire.'

'No!' screamed Gerald. 'You carpet-bagger!' And with that a quick bound into the middle of the darkness, he ran down the hill, leaving the two men standing by the motor-car. He heard them laughing; then he heard them shouting after him and to each other; then he heard them beginning to run after him. He plunged sideways into a hedge, scratching his face and arms and bruising his eye against a thick branch. At last he managed to struggle through the long wet grasses of a field. He could hear the two men running down the hill; they passed within a few yards of him on the other side of the hedge; they passed by. As soon as he had gained breath he began to stumble farther across the field. They should not take him alive, and they should not find the Candidate's letter. So he tore it up into very little pieces and let go a few of them whenever there came a big gust of wind. When they were all gone he felt brave again and wished he had some other papers to tear up and throw away.

It was ten o'clock at night when Gerald, in charge of a policeman, arrived at Number 2, The Parade. The Candidate was out, but Uncle Richard and Aunt Flo were waiting up, worried and anxious and by no means reassured by Gerald's first appearance. For he was nearly speechless with exhaustion; his clothes were drenched and mud-plastered; his arms and face were streaked with scratches, and he had an unmistakable black eye. All the policeman could say was that he had found him fast asleep in a shop doorway along the Mickle road, and that he had been incapable of giving any account of what had hap-pened to him--only the fact that he lived at Number 2, The Parade.

Uncle Richard fetched the doctor; meanwhile Aunt Flo rubbed Gerald with towels, gave him some Benger's Food, and put him to bed with three hot bricks wrapped round with pieces of blanket. He was fast asleep again long before the doctor came.

In the morning he felt much better except for a certain dazedness, aches in most of his limbs, and an eye which he could hardly open. Uncle Richard and Aunt Flo were beside his bed when he woke up. He smiled at them, because they were Good, and he was Good, and Uncle Richard's house was a Good House. They began to ask him what had happened, and when he was awake enough he launched into the full story of how he had been walking along the road when suddenly . . .

'What road?'

'The road to Mrs. Jones's Farm.'

'Jones's Farm!' shouted Aunt Flo, repeating the words in a loud voice so that Uncle Richard, who was deafer than usual some mornings, could hear. 'But what on earth were you doing along that road?'

Gerald dared not mention the letter to the Candidate, because it was a Secret Document, and Secret Documents were not to be divulged even to one's best friends. So he said, in a casual way which he hoped would sound convincing: 'I wanted to see Mrs. Jones and Nibby.'

'Nibby?'

'The cat. A very big cat.' He remembered with disfavour how Mrs. Jones had called it 'a big pussy.'

'Mrs. Jones and her cat!' shouted Aunt Flo. 'He says he was going to see Mrs. Jones and her cat! The Mrs. Jones at Jones's Farm! Did you ever hear such a story!'

'Wuff-wuff,' said Uncle Richard.

'Go on,' said Aunt Flo, warningly. 'And let's have the whole truth, mind. We know you bought some ice-cream off Ulio's cart when he came round in the afternoon, because Mrs. Silberthwaite saw you.'

Gerald did not know who Mrs. Silberthwaite was, but he felt that it had been none of her business, anyhow. He went on, reproachfully: 'You see, a motor-car came down the hill.'

'A motor-car!' shouted Aunt Flo, in great excitement. 'Richard, listen to that! He says a motor-car met him along the road! It would be Beale's motor-car, for certain--there's only the one! Beale in his motor-car knocked him down!'

Now this was not what Gerald had said at all, but he thought it an interesting variant of what had really happened, and he was just picturing it in his mind when Uncle Richard let out one of his biggest and most emphatic 'wuffs.'

'God bless my soul, that young carpet-bagger knocked him down! Knocked the boy down with his new-fangled stinking contraption! Knocked the boy down--God bless my soul! We'll have the law on him, *that* we will--it'll cost him something--wuff-wuff--knocked the boy down in the public highway! Goodness gracious, the Candidate must know immediately! Wuff--immediately! When Browdley hears of all this, young Beale won't stand a chance! It'll turn the election--mark my words--'

And Uncle Richard began capering out of the room and down the stairs with more agility than Gerald had ever seen him employ before. Gerald was excited. His mind was racing to catch the flying threads of a hundred possibilities; meanwhile Aunt Flo was rushing about to 'tidy up' the room; for the Candidate was like the doctor in this, that it would never do to let him catch sight of a crooked picture or a hole in the counterpane.

After a few moments, footsteps climbed the stairs, slowly and creakingly; Uncle Richard was talking loudly; another voice, rather tired and hoarse, was answering.

And so, after those many wonderful days of waiting and dreaming, Gerald at last met the Candidate face to face; and because he knew he was the Candidate he saw what a kind and beautiful face it was, the face of a real knight. Overwhelmed with many thoughts, transfigured with worship, Gerald smiled, and the Candidate smiled back and touched the boy's forehead. Gerald thrilled to that touch as he had never thrilled to anything before, not even when he had first seen the Bassett-Lowke shop in London.

'Better now?' asked the Candidate.

Gerald slowly nodded. He could not speak for a moment, he was so happy; it was so marvellously what he had longed for, to have the Candidate talking to him kindly like that.

'Tell the gentleman what happened,' said Aunt Flo, on guard at the foot of the bed.

'Yes, do, please,' said the Candidate, still with that gentle, comforting smile.

'I will,' answered Gerald, gulping hard or he would have begun to cry. And he added, in a whisper: 'Sir Thomas.'

They all smiled at that; which was odd, Gerald thought, for there could really be no joke in calling the Candidate by his proper name. He went on: 'You see, the motor-car came straight at me--'

'He says the motor-car charged straight into him!' shouted Aunt Flo, for Uncle Richard's benefit.

'Let the boy tell his own story,' said the Candidate.

That calmed them, and also, in a queer way, it gave Gerald calmness of his own. He continued: 'The motor-car came charging into me and knocked me over--'

'Was it going fast?'

'It was going *very* fast,' answered Gerald, and added raptly: 'Nearly as fast as the Scotch Express.'

'He's all trains,' said Aunt Flo. 'Never thinks of anything else.'

But the Candidate showed an increasing unwillingness to listen to her. 'So the motor-car was travelling fast,' he said to Gerald quietly, 'and I suppose you were knocked down because you couldn't get away in time. Is that it?'

'Yes, sir--Sir Thomas.'

'And what happened then?'

'The motor-car stopped and two men got out and came up to me. One of them was wearing a blue badge.'

'Beale!' cried Aunt Flo. 'Didn't I say so? Richard, he says one of them was Beale himself!'

'Please go on,' said the Candidate.

Gerald said after a pause: 'They picked me up and stared at me.'

'Stared at you?'

'Yes. That's what they did.'

'And what after that?'

What, indeed? Gerald could not, for the moment, remember just how everything had happened. But suddenly the answer came. 'They laughed,' he said.

'They *what?*' asked the Candidate, leaning forward nearer to Gerald.

'He says they jeered at him!' shouted Aunt Flo.

'They laughed,' continued Gerald, with gathering confidence. 'And one of them said it was all my fault for being in the way. He hit me.' Pause. 'He hit me in the eye. I ran away then and they both chased me, but they couldn't catch me.' He sighed proudly. 'I ran too fast.'

'Richard--Richard--just listen to that--would you believe it--he says they hit him!'

'Wuff-wuff--my--goodness--wuff--just wait--scandalous--wuff--'

'Tell me now,' said the Candidate, still quietly. 'You say one of the men hit you and gave you this black eye. You're sure he hit you?'

'He hit me,' answered Gerald, with equal quietness, *'twice.'*

Gerald stayed in bed for several days after that, for it seemed that despite all the doctoring and hot bricks, he was destined to catch the thoroughly bad cold that he deserved. For a time his temperature was high--high enough to swing the hours along in an eager, throbbing trance, invaded by consciousness of strange things happening in the rooms below and in the streets outside. Voices and footsteps grew noisier and more continual, shouting and singing waved distantly over the rooftops. Aunt Flo brought him jellies and beef-tea, and Uncle Richard sometimes came up for a cheery word; but for the most part Gerald was left alone, while the rest of the house abandoned itself to some climax of activity. He could feel all that, as he lay huddled up under the bedclothes. But he was not unhappy to be left alone, because he felt the friendliness of the house like a warm animal all around him, something alive and breathing and lovely to be near. There had been nothing in his life like this before. He could not remember his father and mother (they had both died when he was a baby); and Aunt Lavinia, who usually took charge of him during the school holidays, lived in a dull, big house in a dull, small place where nothing ever happened-- nothing, at any rate, like this magic of Browdley streets and Ulio's ice- cream and climbing right to the very top of Mickle.

But the most wonderful thing of all had been when the Candidate bent over him and touched his forehead. As he lay feverishly in bed and thought of it, it all happened over again, but with more detail-- with every possible detail.

'Gerald Holloway, I owe everything to you. If that letter had been discovered . . .' And suddenly Gerald thought of a big improvement: the Candidate was really his father, who hadn't actually died but had somehow got lost, but now here he was, found again, and they were both going to be together for always. They would live in the Parade, quite near to Uncle Richard, and Gerald need never go back to Grayshott except to see Martin Secundus and ask him to come and stay with them. 'Father . . . this is Martin . . .'

And when he grew up he would go on serving his father in the Se- cret Service, because he was more than an ordinary father. He was a Loving Father, like the Father people talked about in church.

The clock on the mantelpiece ticked through Gerald's dreaming, ticking on the seconds to the time when he should be grown up and a man. What a long time ahead, but it was passing; he was eight already, and he could remember as far back as when he was four and Aunt Lavinia hit him for blowing on his rice pudding to make it cold.

But why 'Our Father'? My Father, he said to himself proudly, re- membering how the Candidate had smiled.

So the hours passed in that shabby little back bedroom at Uncle Richard's; but Gerald never noticed the shabbiness, never noticed that the furniture was cheap and the wallpaper faded, never realised from such things that Uncle Richard and Aunt Flo were poor people com- pared with rich Aunt Lavinia in her dull, big house. All he felt was the realness here, and the unrealness of everywhere else in the world.

One morning the doctor pronounced him better and fit to get up. 'His school begins again on Tuesday,' said Aunt Flo. 'Will he be able to go?'

'Good gracious, yes,' replied the doctor. 'Good gracious, yes.'

Till then Gerald had had hopes that somehow the cloud of Grayshott on the horizon might be lifted, that the holidays would not end as all other holidays had done; but now, hearing that most clinching 'Good gracious, yes,' he felt a pin point of misery somewhere in-inside the middle of him, and it grew and grew with every minute of thinking about it.

That night was very quiet and there were no footsteps or voices, and in the morning, when he got up and dressed and went downstairs, he saw that the door of the parlour was wide open.

'Well,' said Uncle Richard, tapping the barometer as usual, 'so here you are again, young shaver.'

There was a difference somewhere. Something had happened. After breakfast he began to ask, as he had so often begun: 'Can Olive and I--' and Uncle Richard said: 'Eh, what's that? Olive's not here any more--wuff-wuff--she's gone away with her father.'

'Gone away? The Candidate's gone away?'

Uncle Richard laughed loudly. 'Don't you go calling him the Candidate any more, my boy. Because he isn't. He's the Member now.'

'What's the Member?'

'It means he's Got In. Margin of twenty-three--narrow squeak--but that doesn't matter. Still, it shows he wouldn't have done but for young Beale's behaviour with that motor-car of his--perfectly scandalous thing--as I said at the time--perfectly scandalous--wuff-wuff--and--consequently was--as I said--it turned the scale. Turned the scale--wuff-wuff--didn't I say it would?'

All this was nothing that Gerald could understand much about, except that the Candidate had gone. 'Uncle Richard,' he said slowly, and then paused. Aunt Flo shouted: 'Richard, why don't you answer the boy? He wants to ask you something!'

Uncle Richard put his hand to his ear. 'Ask away, my boy.'

'Uncle Richard--will--it--all--ever--happen--again?'

'Eh, what? Happen again? Will what happen again?'

Then Gerald knew it was no use; even Uncle Richard couldn't understand. He ran away into the greenhouse and stared through the red glass.

The next morning Aunt Flo wakened him early and gave him a brown egg for breakfast, because he had 'a journey in front of him.' Then he kissed her and said good-bye, and looked at the tricycle in the greenhouse for the last time. Uncle Richard took him to the station and told the guard about his luggage and where he was going. Thump, thump, thump, along the wooden platform; the train came in, actually drawn by a Four-Six-Nought, but Gerald had hardly the heart to notice it.

'Good-bye, my boy. Wuff-wuff. Don't forget to change at Crewe--the guard will put you right. And here you are--this is to buy yourself some sweets when you get back to school.'

Fancy, thought Gerald, Uncle Richard didn't know that you weren't allowed to buy sweets at school; still, a shilling would be useful; perhaps he would buy some picture-postcards of railway engines. 'Oh, thank you, Uncle Richard. . . . Good-bye . . . Goodbye.'

'Good-bye, my boy.'

Gerald kept his head out of the window and waved his hand till the train curved out of sight of the station. Then, as the wheels gathered speed, they began to say things. . . . Grayshott tonight, Grayshott tonight. . . . This time a week ago. . . . This time two weeks ago. . . . Oh dear, how sad that was. . . . The train entered a tunnel and Gerald decided: If I can hold my breath until the end of this tunnel, then it means that I shall soon go to Uncle Richard's again and the Candidate will be there and Olive too, and we shall all climb Mickle together and see Mrs. Jones and Nibby. . . . He held his breath till he felt his ears singing and his eyes pricking . . . then he had to give way while the train was still in the tunnel. That was an awful thing to have had to do. He took out of his pocket the pencil he had poked Polly with (that first morning, how far away!) and began to write his name on the cardboard notice that forbade you to throw bottles on the line. 'Gerald,' he wrote; but then, more urgently, it occurred to him to black out the 'p' in 'Spit,' so that it read 'Please do not Sit.' Very funny, that was; he must tell Martin Secundus about that, because Martin had his own train-joke when there was nobody else in the compartment; he used to cross out the 's' in 'To Seat Five,' so that it read 'To Eat Five.' Gerald did not think this was quite as funny as 'Please do not Sit.' But suddenly in the midst of thinking about it, a wave of misery came over him at having to leave Uncle Richard's, and he threw himself into a corner seat and hid his face in the cushions.

All this happened a long time ago. Gerald never stayed with Uncle Richard again.

Uncle Richard is dead, but Aunt Flo is still living, an old woman, in a small cottage on the outskirts of Browdley--for Number 2, The Parade, has been pulled down to make room for Browdley's biggest super-cinema. The parrot, too, still lives--as parrots will. Just the two of them, in that small cottage.

The Candidate is dead, and Olive is married--to somebody in India, not such a good match, folks say.

The Other Candidate, however, has done pretty well for himself, as you would realise if you heard his name. He is in Parliament, of course, but not as member for Browdley. Indeed, if he ever thinks of Browdley, it is with some natural distaste for a town whose slanderous gossip circulated the most fantastic stories about him once, delaying his career, he reckons, by three whole years. He is very popular and a fine after-dinner speaker.

And Gerald grew up to be happy and miserable like any other boy. He passed from Grayshott to Brookfield, where he became head of house; then he went to Cambridge and took a double-first. But it is true to say that the world was never more wonderful to him than during that holiday at Uncle Richard's when he was eight, and never afterwards was he as miserable (not even during the War) as in the train going back to Grayshott; never did he adore anyone quite so purely as he adored the Candidate, or hate so fiercely as he hated the Other Candidate.

And never afterwards did he tell such a downright thumping lie, nor was there a time ever again when right and wrong seemed to him so simply on this side and on that. A little boy then, and a man now if he had lived; he was killed on July 1st, 1916. When Chips read out his name in Brookfield Chapel that week, his voice broke and he could not go on.

CHAPTER THREE

YOUNG WAVENEY

When Waveney had been at Brookfield for a month he was moved up into the Lower Fourth, Mr. Pearson's form; which was a pity, because he did not like Mr. Pearson. Nor, to be quite frank, did Mr. Pearson like *him*. For Waveney was everything that Mr. Pearson was not; he was young, he was attractive, and he possessed an inexhaustible vitality. Mr. Pearson, on the other hand, was no longer young; he had never been particularly attractive, and he had lately become exceedingly tired. Actually he was forty-three, and owing to a weak heart that made him ineligible for the army, he had come to Brookfield as a wartime deputy.

How a schoolmaster must envy a boy who is obviously going to grow up into a man of much superior personality to his own, and how easily that envy can turn to loathing if the boy senses it and is cruel!

Waveney was not cruel, but he was a passionate hater of injustice, and before he had been in Mr. Pearson's class for a week, that passionate hatred was aroused.

For Mr. Pearson had a *system.* The system, which had served well enough at his previous school, was new to Brookfield; and it was as follows. If anyone in his class talked or fooled about while his back was turned, Mr. Pearson would swing round to try and catch him, but if (being rather short-sighted) he failed to do so, he would say: 'Stand up the boy who did that.' Nobody would respond, of course, because there was a feeling at Brookfield that a schoolmaster had no *right* to ask such a question. He ought to spot offenders for himself, or else leave them unspotted. For, after all, as young Waveney eloquently remarked, if you ride your bicycle on the footpath, you may be copped, but you aren't expected to go to the police station and give yourself up; and all life was rather like that, one way and another.

Wherefore it was manifestly unjust for Mr. Pearson, when nobody made a confession, to pull out a large gunmetal watch, hold it dramatically in one hand, and say: 'Very well, if the boy who did it doesn't own up within twenty seconds, I shall detain the whole form for half an hour after morning school. . . . Five . . . Ten . . . Fifteen . . . Very well, then, you will all meet me here again at twelve-thirty.'

Partly by its detestable novelty, the system worked after a few preliminary trials, and Mr. Pearson's class remained fairly free from ragging. Which, doubtless may be held to justify the system; for Mr. Pearson knew from long experience that, in matters of class discipline, he was such stuff as screams are made of.

Now young Waveney who was about as clever as an eleven-year-old can well be without achieving something absolutely insufferable, had declared war on Mr. Pearson right from the first day, when in answer to a question in a history test-paper--'What do you know about the Star Chamber?' he had written: 'Nothing'; and had afterwards claimed full marks, because, as he said, it was a perfectly correct answer. 'It wasn't *my* fault, sir, that you framed the question badly--what you *meant* to say, sir, was "Write what you know about the Star Chamber"--we like to be accurate about these things at Brookfield, you know, sir.' Mr. Pearson did not give him full marks, but he mentally catalogued him as a boy to beware of; and Waveney mentally catalogued *him* as a poor sort of fish, anyway.

'The system,' however, brought matters to a head. As Waveney urged afterwards to an excited mass-meeting of fourth-formers--'Can't you see that the whole thing's just beastly unfair on everybody? He can't keep order himself, and he expects us to do the job for him. If we don't own up, we're supposed to be letting other people down--sort of honour-bright business--pretty convenient for him, when you come to think about it. Well, anyhow, I warn you, I'm going to make a stand, and I advise all you others to do the same. In future, let's arrange not to own up--ever--when he tries his little game. Let him spot us himself, if he wants to--why should we save him trouble? And if he keeps us in after hours, then let's all put up with it for a time until he gets tired. He soon will. Mind now, not another confession from anybody--we'll soon break his rotten system!'

As it happened, Waveney was himself the first to make the experiment. On the following day, he threw a piece of inky paper while Mr. Pearson's back was turned, refused to confess himself the thrower when the gunmetal watch was brought out, and became thus the cause of a detention for the whole class. The detention took place, and at the end of it Mr. Pearson said: 'Some coward among you has allowed you all to suffer rather than confess his own trivial misdeed. I will give him another chance to declare himself, failing which I shall have no alternative but to repeat this detention every day until Conscience has done its work.'

Afterwards, in rising fury, Waveney told his companions: 'Well, if *that's* his game, we'll see who can stick it out the longest! Only, mind, you fellows have got to back me up! It's hard luck on you for the time being, but I'm breaking the system for you, don't forget that!'

Another detention followed on the next day, and another after that. Young Waveney became more and more tight-lipped about it; he was certainly not enjoying himself, though he was sustained by the feeling that he was leading a moral crusade. After the third detention Mr. Pearson said: 'I am truly sorry for the hardship that some unspeakable coward is inflicting on you all, and if you should happen to know who he is, I don't for a moment suggest that you should tell me, but I have no doubt that you will let *him* know--in your own way--what you think of his behaviour.' It became disappointingly clear, moreover, that Mr. Pearson did not greatly mind the detentions; he read a novel all the time, and as he was a lonely man with few social engagements an extra half-hour a day did not much matter to him.

Unfortunately the fourth form had many social engagements--in particular the annual match against Barnhurst, of which one of the detentions compelled them to miss the beginning. Ladbroke, a keen cricketer (which Waveney was not), said, rather curtly: 'Pity you chose this week of all weeks for your stunt, Waveney.'

After the fourth detention someone said: 'Waveney daren't own up now, he's in too much of a funk--so I suppose we'll all get kept in for ever.'

After the fifth detention Waveney found himself suddenly unpopular, and he hated it. 'Bit of a swine, young Waveney, the way he's carrying on--pity he hasn't got more guts, he'd have owned up long since. Pearson says it's a cowardly thing to do, and I reckon it is, too.'

After the sixth detention Waveney went to Mr. Pearson in his room and confessed.

'Ah,' said Mr. Pearson, who was not essentially an unkind man (especially when his enemy was humbled), 'so you are the culprit, eh?'

'Yes.'

'And it is for you that your classmates have already suffered so much--and so undeservedly?'

'Yes I did it.'

'And you found you could not go on, eh? The pangs of Conscience became too acute--the still, small voice that spoke inside you telling you it was a mean thing to have done, a cowardly thing--isn't that what it told you, Waveney--isn't that why the tears are in your eyes?'

'No,' answered Waveney, nearly howling with rage. 'I think it's nothing but a dirty trap, and it's your rotten system that's really the mean and cowardly thing, and--and--'

Mr. Pearson faced Waveney with a glassy stare. His moment was spoilt. 'Waveney, you forget yourself! And you will go to the Head-master for being intolerably impudent--impudence, sir, is a thing I will *not* put up with. . . .'

So young Waveney was summoned to Chips's study that same evening. Chips was seventy then, recalled from a well-earned retire-ment to assume the temporary headship of Brookfield during the War years. He had been at Brookfield for nearly half a century, and he had known boys rather like young Waveney before. He had also known masters rather like Mr. Pearson before. There was not much, indeed, that Chips had not known before; only the details, the patterned con-figurations of events, were apt to rearrange themselves.

'Well--umph?' he said, peering over his spectacles across the desk and giving his characteristic chuckle.

'Mr. Pearson sent me, sir.'

'Umph--yes--you're--Waveney, yes--umph--Mr. Pearson sent me a little note about you. Some little--umph--misunderstanding eh? Sup-pose you--umph--tell me about it--in your own words?'

Waveney launched into a concise account of exactly what hap-pened (he was really a very clear-minded boy), while Chips listened with an occasional twitching of the eyes and face. When the tale was told, Chips sat for a moment in silence, looking at Waveney. At length he said: 'Bless me, boy, what a chatterer you are--you take after your father--umph--he was president of the debating society--talked the biggest--umph--nonsense--I ever heard! And now he's--umph--in Par-liament--well, well, I'm not surprised. . . .'

After a pause he went on:

'But you know, Waveney--umph--you're not fair to Mr. Pearson. You'd make his life a misery--umph--if you could--and you blame him because--umph--he's found a way of stopping you! Come, come--he's got to protect himself against all you fourth-form ruffians--umph--eh?'

'But it's the system, sir.'

'Systems, my boy, are hard things to fight. I warn you of that. . . . Well, I must do something with you--umph--I suppose. What do you--umph--suggest?'

'I--I don't know, sir.'

'The--umph--usual?'

'If you like, sir.'

'Umph--as if *I* care--so long as *you're* satisfied--umph . . . but there's one thing, Waveney . . .'

'Yes, sir?'

'Be--be *kind,* my boy.'

'Kind, sir?'

'Yes--umph--even when you're fighting systems. Because there are--umph--human beings--behind those systems. . . . And now--umph--run along.'

Chips watched the boy's receding figure as he walked to the door across the study carpet; then, with a half-smile to himself, he called out: 'Oh, Waveney--'

'Yes, sir?'

'What--umph--are you going to be when you grow up?'

'I don't know, sir.'

'Well--umph--I think I can tell you. You're going to be either--umph--a great man--or--umph--a confounded nuisance. . . . Or--umph--both . . . as so many of 'em are. . . . Remember that. . . . Goodbye, my boy. . . .'

After Waveney had gone, Chips sat for a time at his desk, thinking about the boy; then he wrote a note asking Mr. Pearson to come and see him.

CHAPTER FOUR

MR. CHIPS TAKES A RISK

It is the wise man who is often wise enough not to know too much, and in his eighty-second year Mr. Chips had grown to be very wise indeed. Living in peaceful retirement after more than half a century of schoolmastering, it was possible for him to enter his old school well aware that, in mere items of knowledge, most Brookfield boys could teach him quite as much as they could learn from him. 'What *is* a straight eight?' he might ask, innocently, and when a dozen young voices had finished explaining, he would reply, with the characteristic chuckle that everyone at Brookfield had imitated for years: 'Umph--umph--I see. I just wondered how an eight--umph--could possibly be straight--umph--that was all. I thought perhaps--umph--Mr. Einstein had changed--umph--even the shape of the figures. . . .'

He was always apt to joke about mathematics, partly because (as he freely confessed) he had never understood 'all this--umph--$x^2 + y^2$ business.' Nor, with such an attitude, was it surprising that he regarded High Finance with something of the bewilderment (but none of the adoration) with which a South Sea Islander regards a sewing-machine. Indeed he once said: 'Few people understand High Finance, and--umph--the higher it goes, the fewer!' He was certainly not of the few, and whenever he had any small capital to invest he put it prudently, if unadventurously, into British Government securities. Only once did he stray from this orthodox path, and that was when (on the advice of a new and excessively plausible bank manager) he bought a few shares in National and International Trust Limited, a corporation which, in the early spring of 1929, seemed as reliable as its name. One April morning of that year Chips found the following letter on his breakfast-table:

To You, Mr. Chips

'DEAR OLD CHIPS--*Just to remind you that we don't seem to have met for years. Do you remember me? You once thrashed me for climbing on the roof of the Big Hall--that was way back in 1903, which is a long time ago. If you are ever in town nowadays, do please have lunch with me at the St. Swithins Club. I should enjoy a chat over old times.*

Yours ever,

CHARLES E. MENVERS.'

Which was just the sort of letter from an Old Brookfield boy that Chips delighted to receive. He replied that very morning, in his neat and very minute handwriting:

'DEAR MENVERS,--*Of course I remember you, and you will doubtless be glad to know that your roof exploit still holds the Brookfield record for impudence and fool-hardiness. I happen to be visiting London next Thursday, so I will lunch with you then with pleasure. . . .*'

So it came about that Mr. Chips entered the luxurious precincts of the St. Swithin's Club for the first time in his life and was welcomed by a handsome, fresh-complexioned man of middle-age, who had once been a boy with keen eyes and a mischievous face. The eyes were still keen, and to Chips it even seemed that the look of mischief had not disappeared entirely.

'Hullo, Chips! Fine to see you again. You don't look a day older!'

They all said that. Chips answered: 'I can't--umph--return the compliment. You look *many* days older!'

Menvers laughed and took the old man's arm affectionately as they entered the famous St. Swithin's dining-room.

'Never been here before, Chips? Ah well, I don't suppose business often takes you into the City. This is the Cathedral of High Finance, y'know. Why, I reckon there are a dozen millionaires having lunch in this room at the present moment. . . . And I'm one of 'em. Did you know *that?*'

No, Chips hadn't known that. 'I'm afraid--umph--I never had much of a head for figures.'

Menvers laughed again. There was nothing of the conventional caricatured financier about him. He was not fat, bloated, or truculent in manner. He did not wear a heavy gold watch-chain--merely an inconspicuous silver wrist-watch. And he did not smoke cigars--just ordinary cigarettes. Except for a veneer of self-display that was more flamboyant than really boastful he had still the boyish charm that Chips so well remembered. And also (as he proudly confided) he had a pretty wife and one child, a boy. 'Hope to put him into Brookfield in September, Chips. Keep an eye on him, won't you?'

Chips reminded him that he had long retired from schoolmastering and took no active part in the life of the modern Brookfield, but Menvers brushed the implication aside. 'Nonsense, Chips. My spies report that your footsteps are heard on dark nights pacing up and down the old familiar corridors. . . . What was that tag in Virgil you used to teach us--begins *'Quadrupedante putrem'*--ah yes, I remember now-- *'Quadrupedante putrem sonitu quatit ungula campum.'* Have I got it right?'

'Perfectly right,' answered Chips, 'except that--umph--I am not yet-- umph--a ghost, and I was never--umph--a horse. . . . But I'm glad to find you still keep up your classical knowledge. It was never--umph-- so considerable as to be--umph--a burden to you.'

So they talked and joked together throughout a simple but exquisitely expensive meal. Chips found that he still like Menvers, and neither more nor less because the fellow was a millionaire. Nor, in his innocence, did it occur to him as in the least remarkable that a wealthy City magnate should devote two hours of a busy day to reminiscing with an octogenarian schoolmaster. Finally, when they were on the point of shaking hands and wishing each other the best of luck, Menvers said:

'Oh, by the way, Chips, I happen to be on the board of National and International Trust, and I saw your name on our register the other day. . . . Hardly the sort of investment for *you,* I should have thought. Quite safe, mind you--don't think there's anything wrong about it. But what's the matter with War Loan for a staid old buffer like yourself?'

Chips explained about his bank manager's recommendation, to which Menvers listened with, it seemed, a touch of exasperation. 'Those fellows shouldn't take chances--why can't they leave that sort of thing to those in the game? . . . Not, mind you, that I want to give you a false impression. The stock's sound enough. . . . Fact is, I want as much of it for myself as I can get hold of. What did you pay for your packet?'

And Chips, of course, having no head for figures, couldn't remember. But by the time he reached his house at Brookfield that evening a long and (he thought) a quite unnecessarily costly telegram awaited him. It ran:

> AFTER YOUR DEPARTURE I FOUND OUT PRICE YOU PAID FOR NATS AND INTERNATS STOP OFFER YOU DOUBLE IF YOU WILL SELL STOP BEG YOU TO DO SO AND DEVOTE PROFIT IF YOU WISH TO SCHOOL MISSION OR ANY SIMILAR RACKET REGARDS CHARLES THE ROOFWALKER.

Now Chips, had he been a shrewd thinker in financial matters, would have argued: This man wants my stock so urgently that he is apparently willing to pay twice the market price for it. Ergo since he is a financier and in the know, there must be something especially promising about it, and I should do better to refuse his offer and hold on. But Chips was not a shrewd thinker of this kind. He was simple enough to feel that acceptance of the offer was an easy way of obliging Menvers and at the same time benefiting a deserving charity. So he wrote (not telegraphed) an acceptance; and that was that.

April, remember. In June, as you probably won't need to remember, National and International Trust crashed into spectacular bankruptcy. When Chips saw the newspaper headlines his immediate reaction made him write to Menvers a sympathetic note in which he said:

> *'I feel that your generous purchase of my shares was so recent that I cannot possibly allow you to bear any extra loss, however small, that would otherwise have fallen on me. I am therefore enclosing my cheque for the full amount. . . .'*

By return came a scribbled postcard enclosed in an envelope:

> *'I have torn up your cheque. Don't be a damned fool. I could see this coming and I wanted to get you out in time. If you must help me, pray for me. . . .'*

Two days later the arrest of Charles E. Menvers on serious and complicated charges of fraud provided the City with its biggest sensation for years.

Chips, as I have stressed all along, did not understand High Finance. His business code, so far as he had any, was simple--to sell things fairly (though in point of fact he never sold anything in his life except old books to a second-hand dealer), to pay all debts promptly

(which was easy for him, as he never owed anything but gas and lighting bills), and to give generously to the needy (which was also easy for
him, as he was in the habit of living well within his income). Simple--
yes, simple as his life. He didn't understand the money axis on which
the lives of so many people revolve--or stop revolving. What he *did*
understand, however, was the notion that any one of his old boys never
ceased to be *his,* no matter what happened . . . no matter *what* happened . . . and therefore, though he was old enough to find such a duty
arduous, he attended every session of the four-day trial of Charles
Menvers.

He sat for hours in one of the back rows of the public gallery at the
Old Bailey, listening to expositions by counsel, long arguments by
accounting experts, judicial rulings on incomprehensible issues, and
(the only really interesting interludes) the prisoner's evidence under
cross-examination. For Menvers, in that stuffy courtroom, provided
the sole focus of anything even remotely aligned to humanity. The rest
of the proceedings--long discussions as to the interpretation of abstruse
points in company law--passed beyond Chips's intelligence as effort-
lessly as had the '$x^2 + y^2$' of his algebra lessons seventy years before.
All he gathered was that Menvers had done something (or perhaps
many things) he shouldn't have done, but in a game so complicated
that it must (Chips could not help feeling) be extremely difficult to
know what should be done at all. Only one incident contributed much
to the old man's understanding, and that was when the Crown Prose-
cuting Counsel asked Menvers why he had done something or other.
Then had followed:

Menvers: Well, I took a chance.

C.P.C.: You mean a risk?

Menvers: A risk, if you prefer the word.

C.P. C.: And what you risked was other people's money?

Menvers: They gave it to me to risk.

C.P.C.: Why do you suppose they did that?

Menvers: Because they were greedy for the big profits that can only be obtained by taking risks and they didn't know how to take risks
themselves.

C.P.C.: I see. That is your opinion?

Menvers: Yes.

C.P.C.: You admit, then, that your policy has always been to take
risks?

Menvers: Yes, always.

Chips smiled a little at that. But two hours later he did not smile when, after the verdict of 'Guilty on all counts,' the Judge began: 'Charles Menvers, you have been found guilty of a crime which deeply stains the honour of the City of London as well as brings ruin into the lives of thousands of innocent persons who trusted you. . . . A man of intelligence, educated at a school whose traditions you might better have absorbed, you deliberately chose to employ your gifts for the exploitation rather than for the enrichment of society. . . . It is my sad duty to sentence you to imprisonment for twelve years. . . .'

Chips paled at the words, was startled by them, could hardly believe them for a moment. And then (such was his respect for English law and its implacable impartiality) he told himself, as he shuffled out of the court: Well, I suppose it must have been something pretty serious, or they wouldn't have come down on him so hard. . . .

He had asked for permission to see Menvers during the trial but it had not been granted; in lieu of that, he intended to offer what help he could to Mrs. Menvers, and with this object planned to intercept her as she left the court. It had not occurred to him that some scores of journalists would have the same idea, plus a greater knack in carrying it out. He did, however, contrive a meeting at her house that evening. He introduced himself and she seemed relieved to talk to him. 'Twelve years!' she kept repeating. 'Twelve years!'

He stayed with her for an hour, and between them, during that time, there grew a warm and gentle friendliness. 'Charles was a good man,' she told him simply; and he answered: 'Yes--umph--I know he was, the young rascal!'

'Young?' she echoed, and then again came the terror: 'Twelve years! Oh, my God, what will he be like in twelve years?'

And Chips, touching her arm with a movement rather than a contact of sympathy, murmured: 'My dear; I am eighty-one,' which might have seemed irrelevant, yet was somehow the most comforting thing he could think of.

Later she said: 'He's worried about the boy. We were to have sent him to Brookfield next term. Of course that's impossible now . . . the disgrace . . . everybody knowing who he is . . . that was the only thing Charles really worried about. . . .'

'Tell him not to worry,' said Chips.

The next day, from Brookfield, he wrote to the prisoner in Pentonville Gaol:

'MY DEAR MENVERS,--*I understand that you always take risks--even on behalf of others. Take another risk, then, and send your boy to Brookfield as you had in-tended. . . .'*

Young Menvers arrived on the first September day of the following school term, by which time his father had already served a month of the sentence. The boy was a nice-looking youngster, with more than a touch of the same eager charm that had lured thousands of profit-seekers to their doom.

On those first nights of term, despite his age and the fact that he was no longer on the official staff of the school, Chips would often take prep in substitution for some other master who had not yet arrived. He rather enjoyed being asked to do so; and the boys were equally satisfied. It relieved the misery of term-beginning to see old Chips sitting there at the desk on the platform, goggling over his spectacles, introducing new boys, and sometimes making jokes about them. Of course there was no real work done on such an evening, and it was an understood thing that one could rag the old man very gently and that he rather liked it.

But that evening there was an especial sensation--young Menvers. 'I say, d'you see the fellow at the end of the third row--new boy--his name's Manvers--his father's in prison!' 'No? Really?' 'Yes--doing twelve years for fraud--didn't you read about it in the papers?' 'Gosh, I wonder what it feels like to have your old man in quod!' 'Mine said it served him right--we lost a packet through him. . . .' And so on.

And suddenly Chips, following his age-old custom, rose from his chair, his hand trembling a little as it held the typewritten sheet.

'We have--umph--quite a number of newcomers this term. . . . Umph--umph. . . . Astley . . . your uncle was here, Astley--umph--he exhibited--umph--a curious reluctance to acquire even the rudiments of a classical education--umph--umph. . . . Brooks Secundus. . . . These Brooks seem--umph--to have adopted the--umph--Tennysonian attribute of--umph--going on for ever. . . . Dunster . . . an unfortunate name, Dunster . . . but perhaps you will claim benefit of the *"lucus a non lucendo"* theory--umph--umph . . . eh?'

Laughter . . . laughter . . . the usual laughter at the usual jokes. . . . And then, in its due alphabetical order:

'Menvers. . . .'

Chips said:

'Menvers--umph--your father was here--umph--I well remember him--umph--I hope you will be more careful than he has been--umph--lately . . . (laughter). He was always a crazy fellow . . . and once he did the craziest thing that ever was known at Brookfield . . . climbed to the

115

roof of the hall to rescue a kitten . . . the kitten--umph--had more sense--didn't need rescuing--so this--umph--crazy fellow--umph--in sheer petulance, I suppose--climbed to the top of the belfry--umph--and tied up the weathervane with a Brookfield tie. . . . When you go out, take a look at the belfry and think what it meant--umph--crazy fellow, your father, Menvers--umph--umph--I hope you won't take after him. . . .'

Laughter.

And afterwards, alone in his sitting-room across the road from the school, Chips wrote again to the prisoner in Pentonville:

> 'MY DEAR MENVERS, *I took a risk too, and it was well taken. . . .*'

CHAPTER FIVE

MR. CHIPS MEETS A SINNER

When Chips went on his annual climbing holidays he never told people he was a schoolmaster and always hoped that there was nothing in his manner or behaviour that would betray him. This was not because he was ashamed of his profession (far from it); it was just a certain shyness about his own personal affairs plus a disinclination to exchange 'shop' talk with other schoolmasters who might more openly reveal themselves. For when Chips was on holiday he didn't want to talk about his job--he didn't even want to think about it. Examination papers, class lists, terminal reports--all could dissolve into the thin air of the mountains, leaving not a wrack behind.

But he could never quite lose his interest in boys. And when, one September morning in 1917 in the English mountain-town of Keswick, he saw an eager-faced freckled youngster of about eleven or twelve swinging astride a hotel balcony reading a book, he couldn't help intervening: 'I'd be careful of that rail, if I were you. It doesn't look too safe.'

The boy looked up, got up, looked down at the rail, then shook it. As if to prove Chips's point, it obligingly collapsed and set them both laughing. 'So there you are,' said Chips. 'A minute more and you'd have been over the edge.'

'Don't tell father, that's all,' answered the boy. 'I'd never hear the end of it. I once cut my head open doing the same thing. See here?' And he tilted his head as he pointed to an inch-long scar above his right temple.

'What's the book?' Chips asked, thinking it better not to admire such an obviously valued trophy.

The boy then showed the book--an anthology of poems, open at Macaulay's ballad about the coming of the Spanish Armada. 'See,' cried the boy, with gathering enthusiasm, 'it says--"The red glare on Skiddaw roused the burglars of Carlisle." Where's Carlisle?'

'Burghers, not burglars. Carlisle's a town about thirty miles away.'

'And that's Skiddaw, isn't it?' The boy pointed to the green and lovely mountain that rose up at the back of the hotel.

'Yes, that's it.'

'And who were the burglars--burghers?'

'Oh, they were just citizens of the town. When they saw the bon-fires on top of Skiddaw they knew it as the signal that the Spanish Armada had been sighted.'

'Oh, you know the poem, then?'

Considering that Chips had read it to his class at Brookfield for thirty years or more, he was justified in the slight smile that played over his face as he answered: 'Yes, I know it.'

'You like poetry?'

'Yes. Do you?'

'Yes. . . . I wish you'd come in the hotel and meet my father. We're staying here, you know. I want to climb Skiddaw, but he says it's too much for him at his age, and he won't let me go by myself because he says I'd break my neck over a precipice.'

'You probably would,' said Chips, 'if there *were* any precipices. But there aren't--on Skiddaw. It's a very safe mountain.'

'Oh, do come along and tell him that. . . .'

So Chips, almost before he realised what was happening, found himself piloted inside the breakfast-room and presented to Mr. Richard Renshaw, a squat, pasty-faced, pompous-mannered heavyweight of fifty or there-abouts. One glance at him was enough to explain his re-luctance to climb Skiddaw, and one moment of his conversation was enough to suggest that the boy's love of poetry would awake no an-swering sympathy in the father. 'I'm a plain man,' began Mr. Renshaw, expounding himself with great vigour in a strong Lancashire accent. 'Just an ordinary plain business man--I don't claim to be anything else. I'm here because my doctor said I needed a rest-cure--and there's no rest-cure to me in pushing myself up the side of a mountain. So David must just stay down with me and make the best of it. Especially as it's due to him--very largely--that I *need* the rest-cure.'

He glanced at the boy severely, but the latter made no comment and showed no embarrassment. Presently David moved away and left the two men together. 'That boy's a terror,' continued Mr. Renshaw, pointing after him.

'He's not mine, understand--he's my second wife's by an earlier marriage. My lad's quite different--fine young chap of twenty-five-- accountant in Birmingham--settled down very nicely, *he* has. But David . . . well, it's my belief there's bad blood in him somewhere.'

Chips went on listening; there was nothing else to do.

'Been sacked from two schools already . . . a proper good-for-nothing, if you ask me.'

Chips hadn't asked him, but now he did ask, with the beginnings of interest: 'What was he sacked for?'

'Well, from the first school it was for breaking into the matron's bedroom in the middle of the night and scaring her out of her wits . . . and the second school sacked him for an outrageous piece of hooliganism in the school chapel during Sunday service. Isn't that enough?'

'Quite enough,' agreed Chips. 'But what's the position now? What are you going to do with him?'

'I'm damned if I know. What can *anybody* do with him? If school-masters themselves . . . but it's my belief they don't try. I've not a lot of faith in schoolmasters.'

'Neither have I--sometimes,' said Chips.

During the days that followed Chips would have had more and better chances to get to know David if Mr. Renshaw himself had been less obtrusive. He seemed a lonely, unhappy sort of man, and, having found in Chips a tolerant listener, he made the most of his opportunities. Chips could hardly get rid of the fellow at the hotel, and was heartily glad that he was no mountaineer. It was not that there was anything especially unpleasant about him--merely that he was a loud-voiced nuisance, and the more Chips saw and talked with him the more he felt that David, with or without bad blood, could not have found life very harmonious with such a stepfather. Chips wondered why such an ill-assorted pair chose to take their holidays together. The answer came in Renshaw's own words. 'Y'see, Chipping, there's no-where else for him to go. The rest of the family wouldn't take him as a gift--and you can't blame 'em. So he has to stay with me whether he likes it or not. I'm here for my health and he's here for his sins.'

Chips smiled. 'I only hope my own sins will never take me to a worse place.'

'Oh, Keswick's all right, I know. Quite a nice spot for a holiday. But the boy isn't satisfied with a stroll in the afternoon--he's restless all the time--restless as a monkey. Only the other day one of the waiters

caught him in the hotel kitchen tasting all the food out of the pans . . .
of course I had to give the fellow a tip to say nothing about it. The
boy's incorrigible, I tell you. Hasn't even the sense to see what's to his
own advantage. He knows that his whole future depends on what I
decide to do with him during the next few days.'

'Oh?'

'Well, y'see, I promised that if he was a good boy I'd overlook his
disgraceful behaviour at school and put him under a private tutor for a
couple of years--then after that, if he still behaved well, my son in
Birmingham--the accountant, y'know--might take him into his office. .
. . Wonderful chance, that, for a boy who's had to leave school under a
cloud. . . . You'd think it would make him turn over a new leaf, would-
n't you? But it doesn't . . . he doesn't seem to care.'

Which was true enough. David's efforts to impress his stepfather
with any appearance of remorse or future good intentions were, Chips
could see, so vagrant as to be almost imperceptible. Once Chips gave
the boy a lead to discuss the matter by saying, during a casual conversation in the hotel lobby: 'By the way, your father says there's a chance
of your becoming an accountant. . . . It's a good profession, if you like
it.'

'I wouldn't like it,' answered David, with decision.

'What do you want to be, then?'

'An explorer.'

Chips smiled. 'That's not a very easy thing to be, nowadays.'

'I once explored some caves in Scotland. It was easy enough. It was
father who made all the fuss about it.'

'Oh?'

'Just because the tide came up and I had to sit on a ledge all night
and wait for it to go down again. But I didn't find any gems.'

'Any gems? What do you mean?'

'Well, it said in the poem, you know--"Full many a gem of purest
ray serene the dark unfathomed caves of ocean bear." . . . But I didn't
find any.'

Towards mid-September, as the beginning of term at Brookfield
approached, Chips began to feel the familiar willingness to be back at
work. His strenuous month of walking and climbing had made him
feel immensely fit for his years; even Renshaw's conversations could-
n't spoil such a holiday, despite their tendency to become less
restrained and more repetitive. They dealt largely with the trials and
tribulations of family and business life; Renshaw had not been a happy
man, nor--quite evidently--had he possessed the knack of making oth-

ers happy. It seemed that he had lost a great deal of money owing to the War. He couldn't forget it, and Chips, for whom money meant little and for whom the War (then in its third year) was a continuing nightmare, was scarcely interested to hear in great detail how certain properties of his in Germany had been confiscated. 'There never was anything like it,' said Renshaw, mournfully philosophising. 'And I'd put so much into them. That's what the War does.'

Chips could have told him of other and perhaps worse things that the War did, but he refrained.

'And it's nearly as bad over here, Chipping, the way the export trade's going to pieces,' Renshaw continued. 'I'm in cotton, and I know.' And he added, putting the direct question: 'What are you in?'

'I'm in clover,' answered Chips, almost to himself.

Renshaw looked puzzled. 'What's that? . . . Oh, I see--I suppose you mean you sold out in time and can sit back on the profits? . . . Lucky fellow--I wish *I* had.'

'Yes, I think I've been pretty lucky,' agreed Chips, leading the conversation gently astray.

There came the last evening. Both Chips and the Renshaws were to leave the following morning--in different directions, Chips was not sorry to realise. As a kindly gesture towards someone whom he did not definitely dislike (though he was aware that they had little in common), he agreed to visit Renshaw's room after dinner for a final drink and chat. He did this dutifully, listening in patience to the man's renewed plaints against the state of trade and affairs in general; about ten o'clock he thought he could decently take his leave. 'I don't suppose we'll meet in the morning,' he said. 'I'd like to have said goodbye to David, but I suppose he's in bed by now.'

'Not he,' answered Renshaw. 'I packed him off to the pictures to keep him out of the way while we had our talk. There's Chaplin on or something. . . . He can't get into much mischief in a cinema. Ought to be back any minute now.'

'Well, say good-bye to him for me,' said Chips, shaking hands.

But about midnight he was awakened by a tapping at his room door. Renshaw, in nightshirt and dressing-gown, stood outside. 'I say, Chipping . . . sorry to wake you up . . . but David hasn't come back yet. What do you suppose I ought to do about it? Call the police?'

They adjourned to Renshaw's room to discuss the situation further. It was a night of bright moonlight and Chips, standing by the window, could see the full curve of Skiddaw outlined against a blue-black sky. He thought he had never seen the mountain look more beautiful, and he remembered, with a sharp ache of longing, his first meeting with his wife on another mountain not many miles away--the lovely girl whose marriage and death had taken place twenty years before, yet whose memory still lay as fresh as moonlight in his heart. And he knew, in some ways, that it was David as well as the mountain that had made him think of her, for she would have liked David, would have known how to deal with him--she had always known how to deal with boys, and whatever he himself had learned of that difficult art, the most had been from her. He said quietly: 'I'd give him a bit more time before calling the police, if I were you. After all, it's a nice night--he may have gone for a walk.'

'Gone for a walk? At midnight? Are you crazy?'

'No . . . but *he* may be . . . a little . . . In fact . . .' And then suddenly Chips, turning his eyes to the mountain again, saw at the very tip of the summit a strange phenomenon--a faintly pinkish glow that might almost have been imagined, yet--on the other hand--might almost not have been. 'Yes,' he added, 'I think he *is* a little crazy. . . . Do you mind if I go out and look for him? . . . I have an idea . . . well, let me look for him, anyway. And you wait here . . . don't call for help . . . till I come back. . . .'

Chips dressed and hurriedly left the hotel, walked through the deserted streets, and then, at the edge of the town, turned to the side-track that led steeply up the flank of the mountain. He knew his way; the night was brilliant; he had climbed Skiddaw many times before. A certain eagerness of heart, a feeling almost of youth, infected him as he climbed--an eagerness to find out if his guess were true, and a gladness to find that he could still climb a three-thousand-foot mountain without utter exhaustion. He clambered on, till at last the town lay beneath in spectral panorama, its roofs like pebbles in a silver pool. Life was strange and mysterious, nearer perhaps to the heart of a boy than to the account-books of a man. . . . And presently, reaching the rounded hump that was the summit, Chips heard a voice, a weak, rather scared, treble voice that cried: 'Hello--hello!'

'Hello, David,' said Chips. 'What are you doing up here?'

(Quite naturally, without excitement or indignation, just as if it were the most reasonable thing in the world for a boy to be on top of Skiddaw at two in the morning.)

'I've been trying to make a bonfire,' David replied, sadly. 'I wanted to rouse the burglars of Carlisle. But the wind kept blowing it out . . . and I'm tired and cold. . . .'

'You'd better come down with me,' said Chips, taking the boy's arm. A few half-burned newspapers at their feet testified to the attempt that had been made. 'And you needn't worry about the burghers of Carlisle--burghers, not burglars--they're all fat, elderly gentlemen who're so fast asleep at this time of night that they wouldn't see anything even if you'd set the whole mountain on fire. . . . So come on down.'

David laughed. 'Are burghers like that? They sound like father.'

'Oh no. He's anything but fast asleep. He's worried about where you've got to.'

'Don't tell him you found me up here. Please don't tell him. Say I just went for a walk and got lost and you found me.'

'Why don't you want me to tell him the truth?'

'He wouldn't understand. . . .'

'And do you think *I* do?'

'I don't know. Somehow . . . I think you do in a way. . . . There's something about you that makes it easy for me to tell you things. . . . Do you know what I mean?'

On the way down the mountain Chips talked to David quite a lot, and David, thus encouraged, gave his own versions of the escapades that had led to his expulsion from two schools.

'You see, Mr. Chipping . . . it was a line from one of Browning's poems--I'm like that about poetry, you know--a line gets hold of me sometimes--I can't help it . . . sort of makes me do things--crazy things. . . . Well, anyway, this was a line about trees bent by the wind over the edge of a lake . . . it said they bent over "as wild men watch a sleeping girl." . . . I just couldn't forget that, somehow . . . it thrilled me . . . I wanted to act being a wild man . . . but I didn't know any sleeping girl . . . so I dressed up in a blanket and blacked my face and climbed in through the Matron's window . . . of course, she wasn't exactly a girl, but she was asleep, anyway. . . . Oh, she was asleep all right . . . but she woke up while I was watching her . . . and my goodness, how she screamed.'

'And that's what you were expelled for?'

'Yes.'

'I suppose she didn't believe your explanation?'

'Nobody did.'

'Well . . . tell me about the other school. . . . What did they expel you for there?'

'Oh, that was different. . . . You see, there was a preacher who used to visit us regularly and he always used to pray something about the weather--if there was a drought he'd pray for rain, and if there were floods he'd pray for the rain to stop, and so on. Seemed to me he just did it as a matter of course--so I thought it would be fun to find out if he'd really be surprised to have a prayer answered right away. . . . There was a sort of trap-door in the chapel roof just over the pulpit, and one Sunday during the summer term, after there'd been no rain for a month, I guessed he'd start praying for it, and he did . . . so I just opened the trap-door and tippled a bucket of water over him. . . . I thought he might think I was God. . . .'

When Chips and David reached the hotel, the first glimmer of dawn lay over the mountain horizon. Renshaw was pacing up and down in his room, perplexed, alarmed, and--as soon as he saw David--in a furious rage. Chips tried, and eventually was able, to pacify him somewhat. They all breakfasted together a few hours later--David, very tired and subdued, half dozing over ham and eggs. Renshaw was still--and perhaps not without reason--in a grumbling mood.

'I'm damned if I know *what* to do with him,' he said, glancing distastefully at his stepson, and careless whether the boy heard his words or not. 'If only schoolmasters were any use I'd try to send him to another place, but they won't have him, y'know, when they find out he's been sacked twice already. Damned lazy fellows, schoolmasters--take your money and then say the job's too hard for them. After all, that's what they're paid for, to deal with boys--even with bad boys--why do they shirk it? . . . I tell you, I've no patience with schoolmasters--too easy a life, too many holidays--they don't know what real work is. . . . What's your opinion, Chipping?'

Chips smiled. 'Perhaps it's a prejudiced one, Mr. Renshaw,' he answered. 'You see, I *am* a schoolmaster.'

'*What?* Oh . . . I didn't mean . . .'

'Don't apologise--I'm not offended. . . . I should never have told you except that . . . well, I wonder if you'd consider sending David to Brookfield . . . he could be--umph--directly under my--I won't say "control"--let's call it "guidance" . . .'

'Do you really mean it?'

'Yes.'

'Well, I'm sure it's very generous of you. . . .'

'Not at all. It's just that--as you say--schoolmasters oughtn't to shirk their jobs.'

At this point David looked up from his dozing and Renshaw turned to him. 'David--did you hear that? Mr. Chipping is a schoolmaster . . . how would you like to go to his school?'

David stared at Chips and Chips looked at David and they both began to smile. Then David said: *'What?* You a schoolmaster? I don't believe it!'

'I take that as a compliment,' answered Chips.

CHAPTER SIX

MR. CHIPS MEETS A STAR

'Coming out of the Royal Hotel the other day, who should I espy but Randolph Renny . . .' wrote Miss Lydia Jones ambiguously, ungrammatically, but in substance correctly. For it really was Randolph Renny himself, and by identifying him she made the scoop of a lifetime. A pretty long lifetime, too, for she had been doing an unpaid-for social gossip column for the *Brookfield Gazette* for over thirty years. Prim and spinsterish, she knew the exact difference (if any) between a pianoforte solo 'tastefully rendered' and one 'brilliantly performed'; and three times a year, at the Brookfield School end-of-term concert, she sat in the front row, note-book and pencil in hand, fully aware of herself as Brookfield's critical and social arbiter.

She had occupied this position so long that only one person could clearly remember her as an eager, ambitious girl, hopeful about her first and never-published novel; and that person was Chips. She had been a friend of his wife's, which was something he could never forget. As she grew primmer and more spinsterish with the years, he sometimes meditated on the strange chemistry of the sexes that so often enabled a man to ripen with age where a woman must only wither; and when she withered out of her fifties into her sixties, and Brookfield began to laugh at her and the *Gazette* to print fewer and fewer of her contributions, then Chips's attitude became even more gentle and benevolent. Poor old thing--she meant no harm, and she loved her work. He would always stop for a chat if he met her in the village, and he only smiled when, from time to time, she referred to him as 'the doyan [*sic*] of the Brookfield staff.'

Indeed, it was Chips who had given her the scoop about Randolph Renny--a scoop which many a bright young man from Fleet Street would have paid good money for. But Chips chose to give it to Miss Lydia Jones, of the *Brookfield Gazette,* and Miss Jones, faced with something far outside her customary world of whist drives and village concerts, could only deal with it in the way she dealt with most things . . . that is to say, ambiguously, ungrammatically, but in substance correctly.

This is how it had all happened. One August evening Chips had been returning by train from London to Brookfield. The School was on summer vacation, and though he had long since retired from active teaching work (he was over eighty), he still experienced, during vacations, a sense of being on holiday himself. Travelling back after an enjoyable week-end with friends, he had been somewhat startled by the invasion of his compartment at the last moment by a youngish, almost excessively handsome, and certainly excessively well-dressed fellow, who slumped down into a corner-seat breathlessly, mopped his forehead with a silk handkerchief, and absurdly overtipped a porter who threw in after him some items of very rich and strange luggage.

Now it was Chips's boast that he never forgot the faces of his old boys, that somehow their growing up into manhood made no difference to his powers of recognition. That was mainly true; but as he grew older he was apt to err in the other direction, to recognise too often, to accost a stranger by name and receive the bewildered reply that there must be some mistake, the stranger had never been to Brookfield School, had never even heard of Brookfield, and so on. And on such occasions, a little sad and perhaps also a little bothered, Chips would mumble an apology and wonder why it was that his memory could see so much more clearly than his eyes.

And now, in the train, memory tempted him again--this time with the vision of a good-looking twelve-year-old who had almost established a record for the minimum amount of Latin learnable during a year in Chips's classical form. So he leaned forward after a few moments and said to the still breathless intruder: 'Well--umph--Renny . . . how are you?'

The young man looked up with a rather scared expression. 'I beg you, sir, not to give me away . . .' he stammered.

'Give you away . . . umph . . .' Some joke, obviously--Renny had always been one for jokes. 'What is it you've been up to this time--umph?'

'I'm trying to get away from the crowd--I thought I'd actually succeeded. . . . I chose this compartment because--if you'll pardon me for

saying it--I noticed you were reading the paper through double specta-
cles--so I guessed--I hoped--'

'I may be--umph--a little short-sighted, Renny--but I assure you--
umph--I never forget a Brookfield face. . . .'

'Brookfield? Why, that's where I'm going to. What sort of a place is
it?'

Chips looked astonished. Surely this was carrying a joke too far.
'Much the same--umph--as when you were there fifteen years ago, my
boy.'

Then the young man looked astonished. 'I? . . . But--but I've never
been there before in my life--this is my first visit to England, even. . . .
I don't understand.'

Neither did Chips understand, though he certainly--now that the
other had suggested it--detected an accent from across the sea. He
said: 'But--your name--it's Charles Renny . . . isn't it?'

'Renny, yes, but not Charles . . . Randolph--that's my name--
Randolph Renny. I thought you recognised me.'

'I thought so too. I--umph--must apologise.'

'Well, I hope you won't give me away now that I've told you.'

'Give you away? I--umph--I don't know what you're driving at.'

'My being Randolph Renny--that's what I mean. I'm travelling incognito.'

'Mr. Renny, I'm afraid I still don't understand.'

'You mean you don't recognise my name?'

'I fear not. . . . My own name--since you have been good enough to
introduce yourself--is Chipping.'

'Well, Mr. Chipping . . . you fairly beat the band. I reckon you must
be the only person on this train who hasn't seen one or other of my
pictures.'

'Pictures? You are an artist?'

'I should hope so. . . . Oh, I get you--you mean a painter? . . . No,
not that sort of artist. I'm on the films. Don't you ever go to the cinema?'

Chips paused; then he answered, contemplatively: 'I went on one
occasion only--umph--and that was ten years ago. I am given to under-
stand--umph--that there have been certain improvements since then . . .
but the--umph--poster-advertising outside has never--umph--tempted
me to discover how far that is true.'

Renny laughed. 'So that's why you've never heard my name? My
goodness, wouldn't I like to show you round Hollywood! . . . I suppose
you're not interested in acting?'

'Indeed, yes. In my young days I was a great admirer of Henry Irving and Forbes-Robertson and--umph--Sarah Bernhardt--and the immortal Duse--'

'I guess none of them ever got three thousand fan letters a week--as I do.'

'Fan letters?'

'Letters from admirers--total strangers--all over the world--who write to me.'

Chips was bewildered. 'You mean--umph--you have to read three thousand letters a week?'

'Well, I don't read 'em. But my secretary counts 'em.'

'Dear me--umph--how extraordinary. . . .' And after a little pause for thought, Chips added: 'You know, Mr. Renny, I feel--umph--somewhat in the mood of the late Lord Balfour when he was taken to see the sights of New York. He was shown the--umph--I think it is called the Woolworth Building--and when--umph--the boast was made to him that it was completely fireproof, all he could reply was--"What a pity!"'

'Good yarn--I must remember it. Tell me something about this place Brookfield.'

'It's just a small English village. A pleasant place, I have always thought.'

'You know it well?'

'Yes, I think I can say I do. . . . But why--if I may ask--are you going there?'

'Darned if I know myself, really. Matter of fact, it's my publicity man's idea, not mine. Fellow named McElvie--smart man. . . . You see, Mr. Chipping, your English public--bless their hearts--have fussed over me so much during the last few weeks that I'm all in--gets on your nerves after a time--signing autographs and being mobbed everywhere . . . so I said to McElvie, I'm going to take a real rest-cure, get away to some little place and hide myself, travel incognito . . . just some little place in the country--must be lots of places like that in England . . . and then McElvie suddenly had one of his bright ideas. You see, I was born in Brooklyn, so he looks it up and finds there isn't a Brooklyn in England, but there's a Brookfield. Sort of sentimental association . . . you see?'

'I see,' answered Chips, without seeing at all. He could not really understand why a man born in Brooklyn should have a sentimental desire to visit Brookfield: he could not understand why letters should be counted instead of read; he could not understand why a man who wished to avoid publicity should travel around with the kind of luggage that would rivet the attention of every fellow-traveller and railway porter. These things were mysteries. But he said, with a final attempt to discover what manner of man this Randolph Renny might be: 'In my young days we used--umph--to classify actors into two kinds--tragedians and comedians. Which kind are you, Mr. Renny?'

'I guess I'm not particularly either. Just an actor.'

'But--umph--for what parts did you become--umph--famous?'

'Oh, heroes, you know--romantic heroes. Fact is . . . I guess it sounds stupid, but I can't help it . . . I've sometimes been labelled the world's greatest lover.'

Chips raised his eyebrows and answered: 'I have a good memory for faces--umph--and also for names--umph--but in the circumstances, Mr. Renny, it seems fortunate that I--umph--easily forget reputations. . . .'

Thus they talked till the train arrived at Brookfield, by which time Chips had grown rather to like the elegant strange young man who seemed to have acquired the most fantastic renown by means of the most fantastic behaviour. For Chips, listening to Renny's descriptions of Hollywood life, could not liken it to anything he had ever experienced or read about. For instance, Renny had a son, and in Hollywood, so he said, the boy was taken to and from school every day in a limousine accompanied by an armed bodyguard--the reason being that Renny had received threatening letters from kidnappers. 'To tell you the truth, Mr. Chipping, I almost thought of sending him to a school in England. D'you know of any good school?'

'Umph,' replied Chips, thinking the matter over--or rather, not needing to think the matter over. 'There is a school at Brookfield.'

'A good school?'

'Well, I have--umph--some reason--to believe so.'

'You were educated there yourself?'

Chips answered, with a slow chuckle: 'Yes . . . umph . . . . I rather imagine I have picked up a little knowledge there during--umph--the past half-century or so. . . .'

By such exchanges of question and answer Chips and Hollywood's ace film-star came to know each other and each to marvel at the strange world that the other inhabited. It was on Chips's advice that Renny tore some of the labels off his luggage and wrapped up his Fifth Avenue hat-box in brown paper and did a few other simple things to frustrate the publicity he was apparently fleeing from. And at the Royal Hotel (still taking Chips's advice) he registered as plain Mr. Read, of

London, and was careful to ask for 'tomahtoes,' not 'tomaitoes,' and to refrain from asking for ice-water at all. A few days later he rang up Chips on the telephone, said he was feeling a little bored and suggested a further meeting. Chips asked him to tea at his rooms opposite the School, and afterwards showed him over the School buildings. Renny was horrified at the primitiveness of the School bathrooms, and was still more horrified when Chips told him they had just been modernised. But he was pleased and relieved when Chips told him that there had not been a single case of kidnapping at Brookfield for the past three hundred years. 'Before that--umph--I cannot definitely say,' added Chips. 'There were very disturbed times--we had a headmaster hanged during the sixteenth century for preaching the wrong kind of sermon--yes--umph--we have had disturbed times, Mr. Renny.'

'You talk about them, sir, as if they were only yesterday.'

'So they were,' replied Chips, 'in the history of England. And Brookfield is a part of that.'

'And you're a part of Brookfield, I guess?'

'I should like to think so,' answered Chips, pouring himself tea.

The two men met again, several times. One afternoon they lazed in deck-chairs on the deserted School playing-fields; another day Chips took Renny to the local parish church, showed him the points of historic interest in it, and introduced him to the verger and the vicar as a visiting American. Renny seemed surprised that neither recognised him, and uttered a word of warning afterwards, 'You know, Mr. Chipping, you're taking a big chance showing me round like that.'

'No,' replied Chips. 'I think not. There are--umph--quite a number of people in England who--umph--have never heard of you, Mr. Renny. The vicar here, for instance, is much more familiar with the personalities of Rome during the age of Diocletian--he has written several books on the subject . . . while our verger is so passionately devoted to the cultivation of roses that--umph--I doubt if he ever goes to the cinema at all. . . . So I think you may feel quite safe in Brookfield--nobody will annoy or molest you.'

But after another few days had passed and there had been other meetings, a dark suspicion began to enter Chips's mind. Renny looked much better for his rest-cure; idle days in sunshine and fresh air had soothed the tired nerves of an idol whose pedestal too often revealed him as merely a target. All the same, there was this dark suspicion--a suspicion that suggested itself most markedly whenever the two men walked about the streets of Brookfield. Just this--that though Renny was doubtless sincere in wanting to get away from crowds of autograph-hunting admirers, he did not altogether relish the ease with which in Brookfield he was doing so. There were moments when, perhaps, the success of his incognito peeved him just a trifle. It would have been truly awful if a mob of girls had torn the clothes off his back (they had done this several times in America), but when they didn't, then . . . well, there were moments when Renny's attitude might almost have been diagnosed as: Why the hell don't they try to, anyway. . . ?

All of which came to a head in the sudden appearance of McElvie on the scene. This wiry little Scots-American arrived in Brookfield like a human tornado, expressed himself delighted with the improvement in Renny's health, demanded to meet the old gentleman with whom he had been spending so much time, wrung Chips's hand effusively, and opined (gazing across the road at the School buildings) that it certainly looked 'a swell joint.'

'And see,' he added, taking Renny and Chips by the arm and drawing them affectionately together, 'I've got a swell idea, too. . . . I'll work up a lot of phooey in the papers about your disappearance. . . . "Where is Randolph Renny?" "Has anybody seen him?"--"He's hiding somewhere--where is it?"--you know the sort of thing . . . and then, when all the excitement's just boiling over, we'll discover you here . . . spending a vacation with the old professor. . . .'

'I'm not a professor . . .' protested Chips, feebly.

'Aw, it's the same thing . . . and you knew Irving, too . . . and Forbes-Robertson . . . Sarah Bernhardt . . . the immortal Dewser. . . .'

'I didn't know them,' protested Chips, still feebly. 'I only saw them act.'

'Aw, what does that matter? . . . after all, you saw 'em and you're old enough to have known the whole bunch of 'em . . . they gave you tips about acting--and you took in what they said--and now you pass it all on to Renny here. . . . Oh, boy, what an idea--handing on the great tradition--Randolph Renny vacations secretly with Dewser's oldest friend--you were room-mates, maybe, you and Dewser--'

'Hardly,' answered Chip. 'It was--umph--before the days of co-education. . . .'

'Oh, a woman?' replied McElvie, seizing the point with an alertness Chips could not but recognise and admire. 'I beg your pardon, Mr. Chipping--no offence meant, I'm sure. . . . But you got the idea, haven't you?--why it's stupendous--it's unique--I don't believe it's ever been thought of before--Oh, boy, it'll be the greatest scoop in the history of movie publicity. . . .'

Which was why, that same evening, Chips gave Miss Lydia Jones the news that Randolph Renny was staying in Brookfield at the Royal Hotel. He decided that if there were to be a scoop at all (whatever a scoop was), Brookfield, as represented by the *Brookfield Gazette* and by its social reporter, should have it. And thus it came about that Miss Jones began her column of gossip ambiguously, ungrammatically, yet in substance correctly with the words: 'Coming out of the Royal Hotel the other day, who should I espy but Randolph Renny. . . .'

It only remains to add that the following term Renny's son began his career at Brookfield School, and, during a preliminary interview with Chips, remarked: 'Of course you know who my father is, don't you, sir?'

'I do, my boy,' Chips answered. 'But--umph--you need have no fear--on *that* account. We all know--but at Brookfield--umph--we do not care. . . .'

CHAPTER SEVEN

MERRY CHRISTMAS, MR. CHIPS

They say that old schoolmasters get into a rut, that it takes a young man to supply new ideas. Perhaps so; and it is true enough that Chips, in his seventieth year, was giving pretty much the same Latin lessons as he had given in his fiftieth or his thirtieth. The use of--umph--the Supine in "u," Richards,' said Chips, from his desk in the fourth-form room, 'seems to have escaped your notice--umph--and that--umph--can only be ascribed to the Supine in You!' Laughter . . . and if some young man could have done it better, let us give him a cheer, for he is probably doing it better, or trying to--at Brookfield now.

But in 1917, that desperate year darkening towards its close, there were no young men at Brookfield. There was a strange gap between boyhood and age, between the noisy challenge of fourth-formers and the weary glances of elderly overworked men; and only Chips, oldest and most overworked of them all, knew how to bridge that gap with something eternally boyish in himself.

Besides, ideas did come to him--once, for instance, as he was sitting at his desk in the Head's study, that more illustrious desk to which, after his retirement in 1913, he had been summoned as youths were being summoned elsewhere. (But his own service, he often said, was 'acting' rather than 'active'; and that, with the little 'umph-umph' that had become a mannerism with him, was a joke at the expense of his official status of 'acting-headmaster.')

The idea came because a tall air-browned soldier knocked at the study door during the hour devoted to what Chips called his 'acting,' strode colossally over the threadbare carpet, and, with a mixture of extreme shyness and bursting cordiality, stood grinning in front of the desk. 'Hullo, sir. Thought I'd give you a call while I was hereabouts. And I'll bet you don't know who I am!'

And Chips, adjusting his spectacles in a room already dim with November fog, blinked a little, and--after five seconds--answered: 'Oh yes . . . it's--umph--it's Greenaway, isn't it?'

'Well, I guess that's one on me! You've got it right first time, sir! How on earth d'you manage it--Pelmanism or something?'

Chips shook his head with a slow smile.

'No . . . no . . . I just--umph--remember. . . . I just remember. . . .' But he was a little saddened, because he had never taken so long to remember before, and he wondered if it were his eyesight or his memory that was beginning to fail; but perhaps, after all, only his eyes, for he added: 'You were here in--umph--let me see--in nineteen-hundred, eh? Well, how are you, my boy? Umph--you won't mind if--umph--I call you that, will you? . . . Sit down and talk to me. I'm--umph--delighted to see you again. Still--umph--imitating the farm-yard?'

'Goodness--you remember *that*, too? You're a wonder. . . . I've turned Canadian--went out there in nineteen-oh-seven--got my own ranch--found quite a lot of new animals to imitate. . . . Now I'm over with the battalion, and by the freakiest chance we've been sent here to camp. Quite a thriving military centre, Brookfield, just now. I met another fellow the other day who used to be in your fourth form--English fellow named Wallingford.'

'Wallingford . . . there was only one Wallingford. A quiet boy--umph--red hair. . . .'

'That's right--it's still red, what's left of it. He asked me to remember him to you. Too shy to come around. I guess there's quite a few Brookfield men stationed here feel the same. School's a strange place when you've left it a dozen years--makes you feel your age when you don't come across a single face you can remember.'

'Except mine--umph--eh?'

'Sure . . . and you don't look a day older. But I thought I saw in the papers you'd retired--quite a time ago?'

'So I had, my boy. . . .' And then came the little joke about the 'acting service.'

The idea came later, when Greenaway, having stayed to lunch in the School dining-hall, had returned to camp, and when Chips, pleased as he always was by such an encounter, was resting and musing over his afternoon cup of tea. The idea came to him with sudden breathtaking excitement, as a young man may realise that he is in love, or as a poet may think of a lovely line. He would have a party, a Christmas party; there should be no more of that shyness; the men who had once been to Brookfield should meet the boys who were still there; all should meet and mix in the School Hall for an end-of-term party . . . a supper, the best that war-time catering could provide . . . a few songs . . . nonsense for those who liked nonsense, talk and gossip for those who preferred it . . . a few simple toasts, perhaps, and no speeches; nothing formal; everything to make the occasion gay and happy . . . his own party, and his own idea of a party.

It grew bright in his eyes as he thought of it, the details assembled into a rich unity; and by the time he went back to his rooms at Mrs. Wickett's, across the road from the School, it was like good news that he could no longer keep to himself. 'Mrs. Wickett,' he said, when she came in with his evening meal, 'I've had an idea. . . .'

She was rather less enthusiastic than he had hoped. 'Mind ye don't tire yeself, that's all,' she commented. 'There'll be a lot of work arranging a thing of that sort, and if you was to ask me, sir, you're a bit past the age for giving parties!'

'Past it, Mrs. Wickett? Why--umph--I've only just reached it!'

And the smile he gave her faded, as it so often did, into the private smile of reminiscence; he was thinking that he was really the right age because, as a young man, he would have been far too scared and worried to tackle such an enterprise at all. How he had fidgeted, in those days, over whether he ought to put on a white tie or a black tie for some function, whether he ought to shake hands with Mr. So-and-so, whether he would say the right thing in his speech . . . but now, thank heaven, he didn't care, and one of the lovely joys of growing old was to add to this list of trivial things one didn't care about, so that one had more time to care for the things that were not trivial.

'I shall count on you--umph--to help me, Mrs. Wickett. . . . Some of your famous meat-and-potato pies--umph--eh?'

'With war-time flour and strict rations of meat!' answered Mrs. Wickett in pitying scorn. But there were ways and means, and Chips knew that neither wars nor governments would be allowed to frustrate Mrs. Wickett in her search for them. She was *that* sort of an ally.

The next morning the idea was still so strong in him that he dropped a hint to his favourite fourth-form and within an hour the rumour was all over the School--'Old Chips is going to give a party!'-- 'Have you heard the latest--Chips is having a party on the last day of term--a Christmas party'--'Everybody's invited . . . and also some old boys from the camps.' This last was added, if at all, as an afterthought;

for schoolboys are not really interested in old boys, except on speech days or unless they happen to be brothers. Their lack of interest is part of their lack of worry over the future, which is a natural thing--and in 1917 a good thing, too. For then at Brookfield there were boys who were to die within a year; and they were quite happy, playing rugger and conjugating verbs and reading the War news, only half aware that the last concerned them any more than the second, or as much as the first.

So the idea of the party was launched upon a boisterously welcoming world, and in that welcome Chips found more than compensation for extra work; he found a secret sunshine that warmed and comforted him during those sad November days. Indeed, he tremendously enjoyed the planning and discussion and settlement of all the difficult details--the writing of personal invitations, the wheedling of tradesmen into promising precious food, the building up of the whole evening's programme into what, on paper and in anticipation, was already a huge success. And fourth-formers found it enticingly easy, as the term-end drew near, to switch over from conversation about such dull matters as *Cæsar's Gallic War* and the use of the Supine in 'u.' *Ut omnes conjurarent. . . .* Oh, I say, sir, that reminds me, do you think we could have any conjuring at the party? I know a few tricks, sir.'

'Tricks, eh, Wilmer? And evidently--umph--one of those tricks is-- umph--not to prepare your work! "Conjuro" doesn't mean "conjure." . . .'

'I know, sir, but it reminded me. Do you think I *could* do a few conjuring tricks?'

'Well, well--umph--'

And then of course the lesson was ruined and everyone began to talk about the party. But no--not ruined. It was the world, the world outside Brookfield, that was nearly in ruins. Beyond the quiet mists of the fen country men in their millions were crouching in frozen mud, starving and thirsting in deserts, drowning in angry seas and swooping to death in mid-air, fretting in hospitals far from home. So that at Brookfield, even at Brookfield, the Supine in 'u' lost ground as a subject of topical discussion; it gave up part of its ancient ghost, and into that place, unbidden but also unforbidden, came Chips's Christmas Party. It was fun to talk about that, to plan more schemes about it, to lure Chips on to chatting, gossiping, telling you things about Brookfield that had happened years before, things you'd never have known about unless Chips had told you them.

'Do you think Jones Tertius could play his mouth-organ at the party, sir? He's awfully good at it.'

'I could fix the electric lights to make a sort of footlights, sir, in front of the piano--don't you think that would be a good idea?'

'My brother's got a farm, sir, he's promised to send us some real butter. . . .'

And as he sat there at his desk, with suggestions and offers pouring in on him faster than he could deal with them all, he felt that history was not only made by guns and conquests, but by every pleasant thing that stays in memory after it has once happened, and that his Party would so stay, would be remembered at Brookfield as long as--say--the strange revisitation of Mr. Amberley, Mr. Amberley who came back from South America and gave every boy ten shillings to spend at the tuck-shop. 'Umph--yes--Mr. Amberley--a good many years ago that was.'

'Oh, do tell us about Mr. Amberley, sir.'

'Well, you see--umph--Mr. Amberley was once a master here--quite a young man--and not, I fear, very good at dealing with your--umph--ruffianly predecessors. (Laughter.) Your father, Marston--umph--will remember Mr. Amberley--umph--because he once--umph-umph--inserted a small snake in the lining of Mr. Amberley's hat. . . . (Laughter.) Quite a harmless variety, of course . . . and so--umph--was Mr. Amberley. . . . (Laughter.) And then after his first term--Mr. Amberley very wisely went to South America, where--umph--he was much more successful in forecasting the future price of--umph--nitrates, I think it was. So that when he came back to see us he was--umph--quite a rich man. . . . Bless me, there's the bell; we don't seem to have done very much--umph--this morning. . . .'

'But about the party, sir--do you think I *could* fix the electric lights, sir?'

'Well, Richards, if you'll undertake not to blow us all up--'

The day came nearer. Three weeks off. A fortnight off. Then 'Wednesday week.' And on the Thursday the School was to disperse for the Christmas holidays. Brookfield was on rising tiptoe with the pure eagerness of anticipation. When you grow older you miss that eagerness; life may be happy, you may have health and wealth and love and success, but the odds are that you never look forward as you once did to a single golden day, you never count the hours to it, you never see some moment ahead beckoning like a goddess across a fourth dimension. But Brookfield did, and does still; and so, as that autumn term dragged to an end, the tension rose; the Big Hall took on a faintly roguish air with its unusual embellishments of holly and paper festoons; mysterious sounds of practice and rehearsal came from the music-rooms; eager discussions were held in the kitchens between staff and housekeeper and Chips.

Because it was so clearly going to be a grand success. Eleven old boys in the neighbouring military camps had accepted invitations, and four walking cases from local hospitals; fifteen representatives of the Brookfield that Chips remembered, chance-chosen by the hazards of war. And this timely meeting of boys and men, if Chips allowed himself to dream about it, became something epic in his vision, the closer knitting of a fabric stronger, because more lasting than war. He could not have put much of this into words, and would not even if he could; but the feeling was in him, giving joy to every detail. And the details came crowding in. Richards had contrived an elaborate electrical dodge for lighting up the piano. Greenaway would give his celebrated farmyard imitations. And Chips himself told Mrs. Wickett to look over the dinner-suit that he had not worn for years and that smelt of age and camphor.

And then, on a certain Sunday morning in December, an odd thing happened during the School chapel service--in the middle of a sermon about the disputed authorship of one of the books of the Old Testament. Brookfield, plainly, was not interested in the dispute and definitely declined to take sides in it; you could tell that from the rows of faces in the pews. But all at once, quite astonishingly, something happened that interested Brookfield a great deal; Attwood Primus, commonly called Longlegs, suddenly fainted and, after slipping to the floor with a reverberating crash, had to be dragged out by hastily roused prefects. During the last hymn conversation buzzed excitedly, and (to the tune of *For All the Saints*) it was confidently rumoured that Attwood was dead.

Attwood, however, was not dead (and is not dead yet); but he was in the sick-room with a temperature of a hundred and two, and before lights-out that same Sunday evening five others had joined him. The next day came seventeen more. Chips, very calm in such an emergency, sat late in consultation with Merivale, the School doctor. With the result that on the following morning Brookfield was alive with the most intoxicating rumour that even a school can ever have.

'I say, heard the latest?--we're breaking up tomorrow instead of Thursday week--someone heard Chips talking to Merivale--'

'It's the 'flu--it's in all the army camps and Longlegs got it from his cousin, who's in one of them--good old Longlegs--'

'Special orders from the War Office--so they say--Nurse told me--'

'Chips has sent down to the bank for journey money--'

'I say--ten days' extra hols--what luck!'

And--in an instant--in less than an instant--the party was forgotten. Perhaps the conjurer and the mouth-organist gave it a passing thought, perhaps even a thought of wasted planning and unapplauded prowess; but even in them regret was swamped by the overmastering joy of Going Home. Which was only natural. Chips, whose home was Brookfield, knew how natural it was. And so, as he sat at his window in the early morning and watched the taxis curving to and fro through the gateway, he smiled.

He spent Christmas, as he had so often done, in his rooms across the road. There were no visitors, but he was fairly busy. There had been a few details of cancellation to put in order; the promised gifts of food were transferred to hospitals; outside guests were notified that owing to . . . etc. etc., it was much regretted that the party could not be held. But the decorations remained in the Hall, half finished, and Richards's vaunted footlights, in an embryo stage of dangling flex, impeded the progress of anyone who might seek to mount the platform; but no one did. Then the last of the sick-room unfortunates recovered and went home, shaking hands with Chips as the latter doled out money for the train fare. 'Happy Christmas, sir.'

'Thank you, Tunstall--umph--and the same to you, my boy.'

Christmas Eve brought rain in the late afternoon; it had been a cold day with grey scudding clouds. No school bell sounded across the air, and that to Chips gave a curious impression of timelessness, so that when he sat by the fire and read the paper the moments swam easily towards the dinner hour. 'You'll join me, Mrs. Wickett, in--umph--a glass of wine?' he had said, and she had answered, with familiar reluctance: 'Oh dear, I dunno as I ought, sir; it does go to me head so.'

But she did, of course, and in that little room, with the old-fashioned Victorian furniture and the red-and-blue carpet and the photographs of School groups on the walls, Chips made light of any disappointment that was in him.

'Well, sir, if you was to ask me, I'd say it was proper Providence, it was, for it's my belief the fuss of it all would have knocked you up--that it would, and Doctor Merivale said the same, knowin' what a lively set-to them boys was going to make of it.'

'*Were* they, Mrs. Wickett? Umph--umph--well, they're all enjoying their own parties now--more than--umph--they'd have enjoyed anything here--umph--that's very certain!'

'Oh no, sir, I don't think that, sir.'

'Mrs. Wickett--umph--no normal healthy-minded boy--umph--ever wants to stay at school a moment longer than he needs--umph--and I'm glad to say that my boys are--umph--almost *excessively* normal! When is it that they're due back--January 15th--umph--eh?'

'That's right, sir. Term begins on the 15th.'

'Umph--three weeks more.'

After dinner he decided to write some letters, and as he had left an address-book in his school desk he walked across the road through the gusty rain and unlocked his way into the chilly rooms and corridors where his feet guided him unerringly. A strange place, an empty school. Full of ghosts, full of echoes of voices, full of that sad smell of stale ink, varnish, and the carbolic soap that the charwomen used. In every classroom a scrap of writing on the blackboard, words or figures, some last thing done before the world lost its inhabitants. And on a whitewashed wall in a deserted corridor Chips saw, roughly scrawled in pencil, what looked at first to be some odd mathematical calculation:

$$\begin{array}{c} \cancel{17} \\ \cancel{16} \\ \cancel{15} \\ \cancel{14} \\ \cancel{13} \\ \cancel{12} \\ \cancel{11} \\ \cancel{10} \\ 9 \end{array}$$

Which, of course, at second glance he perfectly understood; nay more, he could imagine the joy of the eager calculator when, after that memorable Sunday, the last eight digits of the progression had been spared him! And possibly that same calculator, at this very moment on Christmas Eve, was giving a rueful thought to the date that lay ahead--January 15th--'only three more weeks!' Boys were like that.

He found his book and relocked the doors; then, back in Mrs. Wickett's house again, he wrote his letters. Like most of his, they were written to old boys of the School, and like most letters to old boys they were now addressed to camps and armies throughout the world. Chips was not a particularly good letter-writer. His jokes came to him only in speech; in letters he was always very simple and direct and (if you thought so) rather dull. Indeed, one of their recipients (a much cleverer man than Chips) had once called them affectionately 'the letter of a schoolmaster by a schoolboy.' Just this sort of thing:

'DEAR BRADLEY,

'I am very glad to hear you are getting on well after your bad smash. We have had a pretty fair term, on the whole (beat Barnhurst twice at rugger), but an epidemic of 'flu attacked us near the end, interfering with the House matches and one or two other affairs. We broke up ten days early on account of this. Mr. Godley has been called up, despite his age and health, so we are understaffed again. We had an air-raid in October, but no one at the School was hurt. If you get leave and can spare the time, do come and see me here. We begin term on January 15th. . . .'

Chips wrote several of these letters; then he sat by the fire over his evening cup of tea. All that he had not said, and could never say or write, flooded his mind at the thought of a world so full of bloodshed and peril; and then, in answer, came the thought of those boys who might, by happier chance, miss such peril as carelessly and as cheerfully as they had missed his party. And he prayed, seated and silent: God, bring peace on earth . . . goodwill to men and boys. . . .

'Will ye be wantin' anything more, sir?'

'No thank you, Mrs. Wickett.'

'Happy Christmas to you, sir.'

'And the same--umph--to you, Mrs. Wickett.'

'Thank you, sir. It don't seem long, sir, since--'

Mrs. Wickett always had to say that it didn't seem long since last Christmas, or last Good Friday, or last Sports Day, or some other annual occasion. Chips smiled as she did so--a gentle smile, for there was something in his mind that was always tolerant of tradition. We have our ways, and if we are good folk our ways are fondly endured. 'Time goes so quickly, sir, you 'ardly know where you are. Only another three weeks and we'll 'ave the beginning of term again. . . .'

'Yes--umph--only another three weeks,' answered Chips. And that, of course, was probably what the boys were saying. But Chips, thinking of those lonely classrooms, meant it differently.

THE END

Also from Benediction Books …
Mr. Wicker's Window
- with original cover artwork and BW
  illustrations
Carley Dawson
Oxford City Press, 2011
280 pages
ISBN: 978-1-84902-436-5

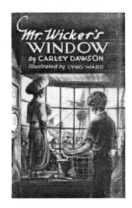

Available from www.amazon.com,
www.amazon.co.uk

This delightful children's storybook, written in 1952 by Carley
Dawson, comes complete with the recreated original cover and it
is fully illustrated. It tells the story of twelve-year-old Chris, who
entered Mr. Wicker's shop to inquire about a job for his friend.
However, he was so intrigued by Mr. Wicker that he took the job
himself. So began an adventure beyond his wildest dreams, full of
magic and adventure.

Hurlbut's Story of the Bible
Unabridged and fully illustrated in BW
Jesse Lyman Hurlbut
Benediction Classics, 2011
976 pages
Size 11 x 8.5 inches
ISBN: 978-1849024556

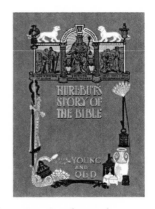

Available from www.amazon.com,
www.amazon.co.uk

In the tradition of parents telling their children stories from the
Bible, this new edition of a delightful book presents a continuous
narrative of the Scriptures that brings the great heroes and events
from the Bible to life. It is unabridged and features 168 stories
from the Old and New Testaments, copious BW illustrations, a
presentation page and a retouched version of the 1904 cover.
Since it was written in 1904 by an American Methodist Episcopal
Clergyman, Jesse Lyman Hurlbut, over 4 million copies have been
distributed.

The Adventures of Sajo and her Beaver People
Grey Owl

Benediction Classics, 2011
164 pages
ISBN: 978-1849024655

Available from
www.amazon.com,
www.amazon.co.uk

Grey Owl's children's story,
first published in 1935. This
delightful novel comes complete with Grey Owl's original
drawings, chapter head-
pieces and a glossary of Ojibway Indian words.

Black Beauty, Young Folks' Edition - abridged with original Illustrations
Anna Sewell

Benediction Classics, 2011
112 pages
ISBN: 978-1-84902-394-8

Available from www.amazon.com,
www.amazon.co.uk

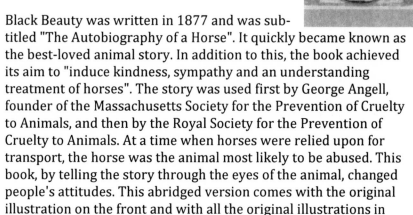

Black Beauty was written in 1877 and was sub-
titled "The Autobiography of a Horse". It quickly became known as
the best-loved animal story. In addition to this, the book achieved
its aim to "induce kindness, sympathy and an understanding
treatment of horses". The story was used first by George Angell,
founder of the Massachusetts Society for the Prevention of Cruelty
to Animals, and then by the Royal Society for the Prevention of
Cruelty to Animals. At a time when horses were relied upon for
transport, the horse was the animal most likely to be abused. This
book, by telling the story through the eyes of the animal, changed
people's attitudes. This abridged version comes with the original
illustration on the front and with all the original illustrations in
black and white throughout the book.

Also from Benediction Books ...
Wandering Between Two Worlds: Essays on Faith and Art
Anita Mathias
Benediction Books, 2007
152 pages
ISBN: 0955373700

Available from www.amazon.com, www.amazon.co.uk

In these wide-ranging lyrical essays, Anita Mathias writes, in lush, lovely prose, of her naughty Catholic childhood in Jamshedpur, India; her large, eccentric family in Mangalore, a sea-coast town converted by the Portuguese in the sixteenth century; her rebellion and atheism as a teenager in her Himalayan boarding school, run by German missionary nuns, St. Mary's Convent, Nainital; and her abrupt religious conversion after which she entered Mother Teresa's convent in Calcutta as a novice. Later rich, elegant essays explore the dualities of her life as a writer, mother, and Christian in the United States-- Domesticity and Art, Writing and Prayer, and the experience of being "an alien and stranger" as an immigrant in America, sensing the need for roots.

About the Author

Anita Mathias is the author of *Wandering Between Two Worlds: Essays on Faith and Art*. She has a B.A. and M.A. in English from Somerville College, Oxford University, and an M.A. in Creative Writing from the Ohio State University, USA. Anita won a National Endowment of the Arts fellowship in Creative Nonfiction in 1997. She lives in Oxford, England with her husband, Roy, and her daughters, Zoe and Irene.

Anita's website:
    http://www.anitamathias.com, and
Anita's blog Dreaming Beneath the Spires:
    http://dreamingbeneaththespires.blogspot.com

The Church That Had Too Much
Anita Mathias
Benediction Books, 2010
52 pages
ISBN: 9781849026567

Available from www.amazon.com, www.amazon.co.uk

The Church That Had Too Much was very well-intentioned. She wanted to love God, she wanted to love people, but she was both hampered by her muchness and the abundance of her possessions, and beset by ambition, power struggles and snobbery. Read about the surprising way The Church That Had Too Much began to resolve her problems in this deceptively simple and enchanting fable.

About the Author

Anita Mathias is the author of *Wandering Between Two Worlds: Essays on Faith and Art.* She has a B.A. and M.A. in English from Somerville College, Oxford University, and an M.A. in Creative Writing from the Ohio State University, USA. Anita won a National Endowment of the Arts fellowship in Creative Nonfiction in 1997. She lives in Oxford, England with her husband, Roy, and her daughters, Zoe and Irene.

Anita's website:
    http://www.anitamathias.com, and
Anita's blog Dreaming Beneath the Spires:
    http://dreamingbeneaththespires.blogspot.com

'AUG — 2013

CPSIA information can be obtained at www.ICGtesting.com
Printed in the USA
LVOW110707111012

302417LV00002B/348/P